International acclaim for LINN ULLMANN's

Grace

"A flawless novel. . . . Linn Ullmann transforms the average into the extraordinary."

—*Frankfurter Allgemeine Zeitung* (Germany)

"A deep rumination on the meaning of life [and] a cautionary tale for those who might think that the word unbearable is easy to define, for the dying as well as for those who love them." —*St. Petersburg Times*

"A masterly tale of death and grace. . . . Ullmann opens doors onto hidden realms within us all."

—*Hufvudstadsbladet* (Finland)

"Graceful. . . . Ullmann handles her material with a light and gentle touch." —*Boston Edge*

"It is merely impossible to write any better than this about death, and perhaps also about love." —*Henne* (Norway)

"A book of rare power, like a drama in three acts . . . where the tenderness is terrible and the compassion merciless."

—*Lire* (France)

"Poignant, thought-provoking. . . . A delight to read."

—*The New Leader*

"A truly great little novel which bespeaks an incredible maturity and knowledge of human nature, not least at life's blackest and most hopeless moments."

—*Morgenavisen Jyllands-Posten* (Denmark)

"Wonderful and chilling. . . . Resonates with a reader's inner, subliminal fears of deterioration in the face of death."

—*Booklist*

LINN ULLMANN

Grace

Born in 1966, Linn Ullmann is a graduate of New York University, where she studied English literature and began work on her Ph.D. In 1990 she returned to her native Norway to pursue a career in journalism, becoming a prominent literary critic. She is the author of the novels *Before You Sleep* and *Stella Descending*, and she also writes a column for Norway's leading morning newspaper. In Norway *Grace* won the prestigious Reader's Prize. Ullmann lives in Oslo with her husband and their four children.

Grace

Grace

A NOVEL

LINN ULLMANN

Translated from the Norwegian
by Barbara Haveland

ANCHOR BOOKS

A Division of Random House, Inc.

New York

FIRST ANCHOR BOOKS EDITION, JANUARY 2006

Translation copyright © 2005 by Forlaget Oktober AS

All rights reserved. Published in the United States by Anchor Books,
a division of Random House, Inc., New York, and in Canada by Random
House of Canada Limited, Toronto. Originally published in Norway as *Nåde*
by Forlaget Oktober AS, Oslo, in 2002. Copyright © 2002 by Linn Ullmann.
Copyright © 2002 by Forlaget Oktober. This translation originally
published in hardcover in the United States by Alfred A. Knopf,
a division of Random House, Inc., New York, in 2005.

Anchor Books and colophon are registered
trademarks of Random House, Inc.

The Library of Congress has cataloged the Knopf edition as follows:
Ullmann, Linn, [date]
[Nåde. English]
Grace / Linn Ullmann ; translated from the Norwegian by Barbara Haveland.
p. cm.
I. Haveland, Barbara. II. Title.
PT8951.31.L56T513 2005
839.8'2374—dc22
2004048601

Anchor ISBN-10: 1-4000-7802-4
Anchor ISBN-13: 978-1-4000-7802-8

Book design by Soonyoung Kwon

www.anchorbooks.com

Printed in the United States of America
10 9 8 7 6 5 4 3 2 1

For Janna Ullmann
(1910–1996)

I

THE WINDOW

When, after an awkward pause, the young doctor delivered the latest diagnosis and began somewhat perfunctorily to describe the various treatment options, never really attempting to hide his certainty that this miserable thing would ultimately kill my friend Johan Sletten, Johan closed his eyes and thought of Mai's hair.

The doctor was a fair-haired young man and could scarcely help it if his violet eyes would have looked better on a woman. He never spoke the word *death*. The word he used was *alarming*.

"Johan!" the doctor said, trying to get Johan's attention. "Are you listening?"

Johan resented being addressed so familiarly. Not to mention the doctor's shrill voice—you would think it had never finished breaking, or perhaps he'd been castrated by parents hopeful of some future for him as a eunuch. Johan had a good mind to make a point about first names and surnames, especially in light of the difference in their ages. The doctor was younger than Johan's son, to whom he hadn't spoken for eight years. But it wasn't just a question of etiquette. It wasn't just that young people should refrain from addressing their elders familiarly as a matter of course. Johan had always been mindful of proper distances. Any intimacy between virtual strangers—like the dreadful custom of exchanging little kisses, not so much kisses as grazings of cheeks—struck him as embarrassing, even downright disrespectful.

To tell the truth, he preferred anyone to whom he was not married to address him as Mr. Sletten. He ached to tell the doctor so but didn't dare; it seemed unwise to create ill will between them at this point. The conversation might take a different tack, and the doctor might start saying unmentionable things about Johan's illness simply in retaliation for having been lectured on matters of etiquette.

"These aren't the results I was hoping for," the doctor went on.

"Hm," Johan said, mustering a smile. "But I'm feeling a lot better."

"Sometimes the body deceives us," the doctor whispered, wondering as he did whether the idea of a "deceitful" body might not be a bit much.

"Hm," Johan said again.

"Yes, well . . . ," the doctor said, turning to his computer screen, "as I said, Johan, there is some cause for alarm."

The doctor delivered a brief monologue explaining the

test results and their consequences: Johan would have to undergo a new course of treatment, possibly even another operation.

When he managed to get the occasional word in, Johan endeavored to persuade the doctor that he actually was feeling much better and that surely they could agree that this was at least a *good sign*, whatever deceit the body might have in mind. But when, in conclusion, the doctor remarked, almost as an afterthought, that this thing was *spreading*, Johan gave up trying. *Spreading* was a word he had been waiting all his adult life to hear—waiting, fearing, and foreseeing. There is no reason, even now that he is dead, to hide the fact that Johan Sletten was an incurable hypochondriac and a catastrophist, and that this scene—a classic of hypochondria—between the doctor and himself had played itself out in his head again and again ever since he was a young man. But unlike the imagination's rehearsals, thoughtfully staged and incessantly reworked, the real scene, the one that actually took place, was hardly dramatic at all.

"Spreading?" Johan said.

"It doesn't mean, of course . . . ," the doctor said.

"Spreading," Johan repeated.

The doctor was quick to point out that this didn't necessarily mean what it meant in the vast majority of cases. That was what he said, more or less. He wanted to give his patient time to digest the diagnosis: he was sealing a man's fate here, after all, and had probably taken courses in empathy, Johan mused.

"How much time have I got?" Johan asked.

"No way of knowing," the doctor answered. "Everyone's different, and, as I said, we have so many options these days—"

"But generally speaking"—Johan pressed—"how long could someone like me live? From a purely statistical point of view?"

"I don't think—"

Johan broke in again. "Okay . . . but what if it wasn't me sitting here? Let's suppose that I am not me and you aren't you. Suppose we are any two people off the street and you, who would of course not be you, are asked to give an opinion, just in the most general terms. What would you say then?"

"As I said, I'd rather not—"

Johan banged the desktop with his fist. "Time! Give me an honest answer; give me something I can relate to. How much time have I got? Don't you see?" Johan thrust his watch under the doctor's nose. "I need to know how much time I've got."

The doctor didn't flinch. He capitulated, looking Johan in the eye. "Six months, maybe more, maybe less," he said. And then, after a pause: "But as I mentioned earlier . . ." He left the sentence unfinished.

There was silence. Johan looked at the floor, plucking gently at his right eyebrow, a childhood habit that lent him a rather wry aspect, a bushy eyebrow on the left and a bald one on the right. He tried to gauge exactly what he was feeling. The doctor's words could not be retracted, but they were just words, not blows or caresses, and words take longer to make themselves felt. He had, as he'd declared, been just fine for a week now, surprisingly vigorous in fact. There was nothing to stop him from getting up and leaving the doctor's office. He could take a walk downtown and step into a bookshop or a music store, maybe treat himself to something special, or just have a look around. No one had overheard his conversation with the doctor. It could be their secret, and everything would be as before. A walk downtown would cheer him up and refresh him; the doctor's office was hot and stuffy, and the doctor smelled of sweat, which Johan had detected the minute he walked in.

He stood up and said, "I can't think straight. I have to go. Let's talk about this later."

The doctor nodded.

Johan said, "My wife will help me with this." And again he thought of Mai's hair, which (and this was the strange thing) lit up a dark room.

Mai was Johan's wife, his wife number two. Wife number one had been Alice. In stressful situations such as this, Johan thought both of his first wife and of his second.

He tried to hold on to the thought of Mai, but something inside him forced him to think of Alice.

Yes, Alice.

The itch.

.   .   .

Johan and Alice were married in 1957. Johan was twenty-five and Alice twenty-six. Two years later, their son, Andreas, was born.

It was an unhappy marriage. Many people complain about their unhappy marriages; many write about their unhappy marriages. Frequently a marriage is said to be unhappy because a deathly hush has fallen between man and wife. That, however, had not been the case with Johan and Alice. Their marriage was a noisy affair, without hush, deathly or otherwise.

Johan often thought that if Alice had not, after twenty years of marriage, been run over and silenced at last by a black station wagon in downtown Oslo, he would have had to run her over himself.

Once, a long time earlier, Alice had hovered, teetering, on the edge of a dock. She couldn't swim, never having dared to try to learn as a child after two little girls, the same age as herself, had pushed her into a pool of water—of no great depth, just melted snow in a ditch—and held her head under until, with sudden and desperate strength, she broke free and ran away. And now here she was, a grown woman, Johan's wife number one, standing on the edge of that dock and basking in the sun.

He could never really explain what made him do it, but all at once he put his hand on her back and pushed—not a gentle nudge but a hefty shove that had the expected effect. Alice fell into the water with a shriek, more surprised than scared, really, as he noted with some interest. Straightaway he jumped in after her and hauled her back onto dry land, unhurt but screaming bloody murder.

"What did you do that for? Are you crazy?" she shouted, water dripping off her face.

She wept, she screamed, she lashed out, her dress plastered to her body, water streaming from her hair, her cheeks, her eyes. Her right shoe was gone, kicked off in the water. She hobbled around the dock, bewildered and forlorn, looking—as he thought with some relish—a bit like a headless chicken.

She planted herself in front of him, made a fist, and punched him in the eye.

"Why did you push me in the water, Johan?"

"I . . . don't know. I'm sorry. I don't know what came over me." He put a hand to his eye. Later it would turn blue, purple, yellow.

She wasn't about to back down. "Why, Johan?"

"I don't know, Alice." He tried to think clearly, tried to come up with an explanation as to why he had pushed his wife over the edge.

Finally he said, "I think . . . I think I did it because I love you."

They stood there, perfectly still, looking at each other, he with just the one eye. Then she bent down and slipped off her left shoe and threw that, too, into the water. Barefoot, she walked away from the dock. Johan stayed where he was, gazing after her. When she turned and called to him, she smiled.

. . .

He used to call her the Horse. When she plopped herself down, for instance, ranting and raving, all that weight landing next to him on the sofa, where he liked to sit quietly minding his own business—it was a little like dozing on a peaceful beach and suddenly being surprised by one of those huge waves that sweep away entire villages. Or when she laughed, baring her front teeth. The sight of those front teeth made Johan feel he'd married a horse. On those rare occasions when he came across a real horse, he would beg its forgiveness. Horses were beautiful creatures, Johan thought, undeserving of comparison to his wife number one.

But when she turned and called his name, all barefoot and dripping, Alice hadn't reminded him of a horse. It wasn't just her smile; it was the laughter in her eyes and the way that laughter purled its way deep into his heart. The thought came to him, unfamiliar and unbidden, that she was still the prettiest woman in the world.

There was always this business about money, though. They had hardly any at all, but she had a bit more than he did. When they were broke her father gave her cash—not a lot, just enough to pay the odd bill and buy food. Once, after they had cooked and eaten an expensive dinner with some good wine and a delicious dessert, all courtesy of her father, she turned abruptly to Johan and said, "I've bought you. You're bought and paid for. You do know that, don't you?"

He never forgot it.

When Alice's father died and left her 150,000 kroner,

Johan suggested that they get a divorce. Their son was almost grown anyway. He said, "You and Andreas can manage without me now." But she went all sweet and soft on him, saying, "Who cares about money, Johan! Forget the money. Forget all of that. From now on we're going to live like kings. You can have whatever you want."

And then, as luck would have it, she got run over.

Many people mourned Alice's passing. Johan was surprised to discover that she was adored. She had been pretty, of course, not to mention young, too young to die, people said. That's what they always say about anyone who dies before a certain age. Everyone under seventy-five, it seems, is too young to die; when it's someone under forty-five, it's called a tragedy, a terrible and senseless tragedy. Alice was well under seventy-five and not much over forty-five. A parade of people clasped Johan's hand, whispering that Alice's death was a terrible and senseless tragedy. Every single time he had to suppress the urge to shout, No, it wasn't! You have no idea! She tormented me!

Their son, Andreas, no doubt suffered the most.

In the days following the funeral, Johan tried to get through to this heartbroken, still pimply stranger who called him Pappa. He made several visits to his son's tiny apartment, occasionally taking him out to dinner. Once they even went skiing on a Sunday afternoon. Then one day, over steak and french fries at Theatercaféen, the boy looked up at his father and said, "Pappa!"

Johan nodded. There it was again: a slightly contemptuous smile. The word *Pappa*, or *Daddy*, or *Father*, or *Pa*, couldn't be said without at least one of them cracking this smile, but Johan couldn't say for sure where the contempt had first shown itself, in his son's smile or his own.

"Pappa," Andreas said again.

"What's on your mind, son?"

Johan laid his knife and fork on his plate, giving Andreas his attention. Always the same thing. Conversations that went nowhere. The boy was incapable of finishing a thought.

"I don't know," Andreas answered. "I'm sure there is— there *is* something I want to say. I just can't seem to get it out."

As a child, Andreas was as spindly as his father. There was something transparent and brittle about the boy's frame.

Alice once said that their son reminded her of an amoeba. Maybe it was Andreas's amoebic appearance that made other children want to hit him.

Johan believed himself generally unlucky with people—at least until he met his wife number two, Mai. It was like that song, she reminded him of that song . . . although maybe one shouldn't mix songs and love. Most of the time it's hard to tell which is which. I sometimes wonder whether this thought crossed Johan's mind during the last days of his life. Had he in fact mistaken his romance for a song?

> *Oh, who comes rowing in on the foam?*
> *A maiden, Herr Flinck, in a boat all alone!*
> *The wind, the nor'wester, gives tongue!*

> *Who is this maid, like a man rowing there?*
> *'Tis Maj from Malö, so slender and fair.*
> *But hark to my wonderful song.*

Mai and Johan were married in the spring of 1979, two years after Alice's death. Mai was thirty years old, and Johan was forty-seven. It would never have occurred to Johan to compare Mai to a horse—or, for that matter, to any other creature. Johan could describe her only as his grace.

Years before, when Mai was a girl, her ambition was to become a concert pianist. But her father, a musician himself, dissuaded her. Mai wasn't gifted, he said, she was *almost good enough*. And *almost* wouldn't do, not for Mai and not for Mai's father. So she went to medical school instead.

She still played the piano now and then. Schumann was her favorite, but it was only for fun, she would say, not serious. Mai was always careful to keep separate what was fun and what was serious.

"There you are," she said. "That was my dream, to play the piano. But I had no talent. I was pretty good, but I never would have been *really* good. I didn't have . . . you know"—Mai fluttered her fingers in front of her face—"I wasn't . . ."

"Graced?"

"I don't like that word. It's more . . ."

"You're my grace. I'm graced because you chose me."

"Oh, shush, Johan. Can't we just take one day at a time and try to avoid these grand statements?"

One sunny day not long after Mai and Johan met, Johan took a picture of her. In it she's sitting on a bench in Frognerparken. She's wearing blue jeans, and her long, fair hair is twisted up into a knot.

In those days she had bangs and, despite her thirty years, seemed as if she had just turned nineteen. This sometimes led to rather comical situations at work: Mai the pediatrician, occasionally mistaken for a child herself.

In the photograph she looks pale, even wan. She has brown eyes, a full lower lip, and a large hooked nose. She was ashamed of her nose as a girl, but the older she got, the less it bothered her. Her face seemed to have risen to the task of carrying such a nose, as if it were a valuable piece of jewelry, a family heirloom.

"She wears her nose like Bette Davis wore that mink coat in *All About Eve*—with the same nonchalant femininity," Johan once said.

Hardly a day went by that he didn't look at that picture of Mai. But he showed it only once. Bursting with happiness because this woman had agreed to live with him and sleep with him, he had taken it out in front of three colleagues who were also his only three friends. Johan wrote for a leading

Norwegian newspaper. He had recently applied for the position of arts editor, only to be passed over in favor of a literary dilettante generally referred to around the office as the fool. The editor in chief had reportedly said that Johan was "far too weighed down by grief" after Alice's tragic death, and even now, two years later, nowhere near ready to do something as important and demanding as editing the arts section of Norway's third biggest-selling newspaper. He did not know that, for Johan, Alice was nothing but an itch, now that his life had been graced by Mai.

So it was not as Norway's third most important arts editor that Johan sat with his three colleagues, his only friends, around a table in a café, drinking beer and discussing a new novelist, a young woman everyone said was tremendously gifted. Suddenly, with a triumphant look on his face, Johan slapped the photograph of Mai down on the table. The three colleagues (Ole Torjussen, Geir Hernes, and Odd Karlsen—fair-to-middling journalists all; Ole Torjussen is dead now) bent over the picture and squinted at it in bewilderment. They all misunderstood, taking Mai to be the new novelist. As I said, she looked very young in that picture. Then Ole Torjussen, or it might have been Odd Karlsen, moaned, "Well, she's no beauty, that's for sure!" And Geir Hernes stifled a fit of coughing and declared, "If you ask me, the least we can expect of this country's new women writers is that they be beautiful. The dogs, like this one here"—he planted a bitten fingernail, yellow with nicotine, on Mai's face—"ought to be rejected at birth."

Johan grabbed the picture, his cheeks burning. He

wanted to wail, as if he were a child again and had just tipped a whole bucketful of wild strawberries into the stream. But he contained himself and didn't say a thing. Ole Torjussen, Geir Hernes, and Odd Karlsen didn't notice that anything was wrong; they'd all had a drink or two. A moment later, the new woman novelist and the picture of Mai were forgotten.

Johan never bothered to clear up the misunderstanding. It later occurred to him that he could have said, "It's the way she moves." He could have said that when she swept her hair back from her forehead she drew the heavens down to her, and how can you not follow the heavens?

If he had been a fighting man, he would have fought. He would have jumped up and punched Geir Hernes in the face. He would have knocked him out cold, not so much for what he had said as because he had touched Mai's face, and to this day the photo bears the faint smudge of that pudgy finger-tip. But Johan wasn't a fighting man. He didn't fight with other men, and he didn't fight with his two wives—either the dead one he despised or the living one he adored—and he didn't fight in the columns of the newspaper. When he retired at the age of sixty-four, it was with a sense of never having written anything worthwhile. He wasn't just being modest. His colleagues and readers would have agreed.

When he was younger, he *had*, in fact, written a series of articles that caused quite a stir in academic and literary circles. These six pieces—some described them as essays— appeared with no little fanfare on the newspaper's arts page on six consecutive Saturdays. The subject was William Faulkner: the man, the writer, and the myth. Johan compared American literature and society with Norwegian literature and society in subtle and telling ways. It was brilliant work. Each article took up two whole pages and was thoughtfully illustrated with old photographs. Never had Johan received so much attention from those whose good opinion he valued. He was inundated with telephone calls from doyens of the arts, ringing to say that he had shed new light on Faulkner's work and set a new standard for literary criticism. Johan Sletten's informed and highly personal discussion of Faulkner's life and work had, in fact, said something about the very *art of reading*.

But that was a long time ago. No one mentioned the series anymore. No one talked to him about the *art of reading*. The University of Oslo occasionally held seminars on William Faulkner, but Johan Sletten was never invited to attend.

And now his rapport with the newspaper readers of Norway was history. It was time for him to retire. Although to say that he *retired* is a pretty way of putting it. He was asked to leave. You might say he was fired, sacked, given the boot.

It all started the day a German review of an obscure Latvian novel sparked his curiosity. Johan—and this was not emphasized strongly enough at his funeral—had an inquiring nature. He bought the Latvian novel in a Danish translation, read it, and wept. He wanted to tell everyone in

Norway, or at least all of his newspaper's readers, to rush out and buy this book. But when he sat down to write, he could not find the words to do it justice. They were pale and puny and meaningless, like those innocuous little flies that take on waspish coloring in order to look more fierce. It was awful. His every word trivialized this book he wished to extol. So he did something he had never done before: he translated the German review, put his own name on it, and turned it in. This review, which Johan had read in a literary journal with a circulation of only about fifteen hundred, was by any standard brilliant. It was signed only J.I.S.—they might almost have been his own initials; he just didn't have an *I* in his name. The point was that J.I.S. expressed exactly what Johan felt when he read the book, and J.I.S. got his point across without resorting to sentimentalism, something Johan abhorred above all else, something far too prevalent in the press as it was. J.I.S.'s review was witty and relevant, placing the Latvian novel in its proper historical, political, and emotional context. It was deeply personal and utterly universal. It was, quite simply, the review he himself would have written.

The next day at 1:07 p.m., just a few hours after Dolores, a gorgeous twenty-three-year-old intern, had praised him for having written "the best piece of the year," Johan got an e-mail from the editor in chief asking if he could possibly present himself, without too much delay, in his office for *a word*.

And so it was over.

. . .

You wait all your life for this very thing to happen, and then it happens: you are found out and it's over. Johan took a deep breath.

It appeared that an outraged reader from Mo i Rana was one of the fifteen hundred people in the world who actually subscribed to the German literary periodical, and probably the only person in Scandinavia who knew who the initials J.I.S. stood for. This outraged reader spotted the plagiarism straightaway and wrote a lengthy irate fax to the editor in chief, with copies to the arts editor and the Op-Ed desk. Johan Sletten had stolen J.I.S.'s review. Such a thing was unheard-of, and *this* in an organ that called itself a quality newspaper!

Johan scanned the editor in chief's face. He wasn't angry. In retrospect, Johan would go so far as to say that he didn't even seem surprised. The man did not like Johan, and Johan had done no more than the editor in chief expected of him.

But no—now I'm going too far. If it could only be said that he disliked Johan.

The truth is that Johan was merely a staff member whom the paper wanted to be rid of. He was surplus, and so this act of plagiarism—Johan's one and only, for, mind you, while no brilliant journalist, he could at least be depended upon, and in forty years with the paper, this review of a small Latvian novel stolen from an even smaller German literary magazine (886 words, 4,250 characters) had come as something of an opportunity for Johan's bosses. An embarrassment for the newspaper, to be sure, as the editor in chief did not neglect to inform Johan. The Op-Ed editor had had to spend almost half an hour placating the outraged reader, who was demanding to have his letter printed—it was not a letter, he hollered, it was a *commentary*!—and had to be persuaded that it was an ignoble thing to denounce a washed-up journalist who was due to retire very shortly anyway.

Johan's last memory of that day was this:

Dolores, the gorgeous summer intern, knows nothing of his shame. Everyone else does. The editors, the switchboard ladies, the secretaries, the receptionist, everyone in archives, the reporters, even the guys on the sports desk know—he's the talk of the office now—but Dolores knows nothing. Johan walks down the corridors with everyone knowing, everyone staring at him. He's been waiting for these stares all his life; he knows these looks and has always known that one day they would be directed at him. This is not the look one gives to a man who is controversial. A controversial man meets the eyes of the other, his own eyes saying, I stand up for what I believe in, I stand up for what I've done. But plagiarism isn't controversial. You can't stand up for that.

Dolores was alone in knowing nothing. This utterly stupid, luscious little girl stood before him in the endless corridor. She smiled. She rummaged through the large black bag slung over her shoulder, pulled out the Danish translation of the small Latvian novel, and said, "It's not often a review in the newspaper sends me running out to buy a book." She uttered the word *newspaper* with a scornful, conspiratorial whisper, as if to second Johan's assumed contempt for the low intellectual level of the dailies. "But your piece did," she said, fixing her brown eyes on Johan. "Your piece moved me."

God bless Dolores. He stroked her hair. Nothing like this had ever happened to him before. Not many men have the good fortune to be looked up to by a gorgeous young woman, let alone one named Dolores. For a moment Johan Sletten forgot, made himself forget, the mess he was in.

Gorgeous young Dolores looked up at him, and he stroked her hair, which was possibly even more beautiful than Mai's, and she let him do it.

He got out of there before she found out. He couldn't stand the thought of seeing her again, seeing the look in her eyes after someone had taken her aside and whispered it in her ear. He couldn't face her after that. His life had never been what one might call the picture of dignity. But having to face Dolores again? That was one indignity to which he would not submit.

Instead, Johan accepted the editor in chief's offer of early retirement, never to set foot inside the newspaper offices again.

. . .

Mai was younger than Johan. When they met, Mai was thirty. When he died, she was fifty-three.

During his last months he had a large boil on his left cheek.

One time he asked her for a mirror, and she produced a compact from her bag.

"I don't know what you see in me," he said. "I'm old and ugly and I'll be dead soon."

"But you're still my Johan, and I love you," she said softly.

It often occurred to him. She was his grace, but he was her burden. *But you're still my Johan, and I love you.* A child could have been their shared burden, but she did not want that child. All she wanted was Johan.

On the evening of the day he lost his job, he told Mai about the plagiarized review. He was lying in bed, and she was standing in front of the mirror brushing her long hair, now completely gray but still thick and shiny.

"How come you have such beautiful hair?" he had asked her once.

"Because I brush it a hundred times every morning and every night. First I bend over—like this!" she said, bending over to demonstrate. "I brush from the back, one-two-three-four-five-six-seven, and so on all the way up to a hundred. There!"

That's what she was doing when he told her about the

review. Bending over, listening, counting the deliberate strokes of the brush through her hair.

When he finished his story, she still had thirty-eight to go, and these she completed, slowly, intently, without saying a word. Then came the moment Johan usually loved: the moment she tossed her hair back, letting it fall into place around her face and shoulders. Then she would look at herself in the mirror and smile.

But on this particular evening, when he told her about the plagiarized review, she didn't linger in front of the mirror, smiling.

Instead, still facing the mirror, she said, "Poor you. My poor Johan." Then she turned around, crossed the room, and sat down on the bed. The stuff of her nightgown was filmy and blue, dotted with little white stars. Her feet were bare. She smelled nice. Johan rested his head on her shoulder.

"Do you despise me, Mai?"

"Never," she said, putting her arms around him. "Never!"

An almost identical scene was enacted five years later when he told her about his visit to the doctor. Mai was bending over in front of the mirror—the brush, one-two-three-four-five-six-seven-eight times, through her hair, Johan lying in bed, searching for the right words. Should he tell her about the doctor's office, small and claustrophobic, or about the doctor who smelled of sweat and was younger than his own son? Should he tell her about the word *alarming* and how this thing was *spreading*? He looked at her and thought, She'll help me. She'll put her arms around me and tell me she loves me. She'll put her arms around me and tell me that she'll help me when the time comes. To be allowed to die at the moment of his own choice. To die without unbearable pain. It all came down to dignity, and his life had never been the picture of that.

He looked at her again, standing in front of the mirror. Didn't know exactly where to begin. Couldn't find the words.

The night before Johan's father died, he was found crawling naked on all fours through their neighbor's garden, leaving a trail of shit behind him. The next morning, when his father learned what he had done, he cried with shame, clutched his wife's arm, and begged her to forgive him.

Johan was fifteen years old.

"Stay with me!" Johan's father pleaded. He clutched at Johan's mother's arm. "Don't leave me, Agnes, please!"

His mother shut her eyes tight and shook her head.

"No, don't go!" he cried. "You can't . . . Please, I beg you. . . ."

"But I can't take this," his mother whispered, and she left the room.

It was then that Johan's father began to howl.

The door was shut.

Johan's mother, Johan's older sister, and Johan sat on the sofa in the living room. The lights were off, the door shut.

His father howled. Hour after hour he howled. And then, finally, there came a couple of bellowed cries for help.

Once upon a time, long before he fell ill, Johan's father had painted the bedroom door blue. His mother felt there was something not quite proper about a blue bedroom door. Particularly when, in front of the children and a neighbor who just happened to have popped in, he grabbed her around the waist and declared, "See, Agnes! There's our door to heaven!"

Now the door was shut, the blue paint flaking, and his father howling.

When Johan began to cry, his mother raised her hand and stroked his head. Then his sister raised her hand and stroked his head. Johan huddled on the sofa, between a mother and a sister stroking his head, and listened to his father howling. When the women's caresses did not still his sobs, his mother laid her hands over his ears and pressed the sound out of existence. Then his sister did the same, one hand over each ear. First his mother's hands, then his sister's hands over his ears. And so they sat: Johan in the middle, with his mother's hands over his ears and his sister's hands over their mother's.

It took a while. No one moved. No sounds now. Just the blue door and four hands, women's hands, two pairs of large, warm, dry palms, twenty fingers locked around his ears. Their bodies close to his. Hour after hour. His mother smelled of detergent, his sister of sweat, but only faintly. And then it was over. Johan knew it was over, because suddenly the two women pulled their hands off his ears—*pop!*—

like a cork leaving the neck of a wine bottle. And then: only silence.

Johan's mother got up, crossed the room, and opened the blue door. She stood on the threshold for a moment first, seeming to look about her, as if this were the first time she had seen her own bedroom. The light coming in through the window. The blue curtains. The mahogany bureau with the brass knobs. The big double bed with the blue bed linen under which, when he was younger, Johan had loved to curl up and hide. The constant, drowsy warmth of his parents' bed. His mother called to his sister, and together they managed to lift the dead man onto a rug in the hallway. Then they set to work with brushes and brooms, scrubbed the floor and walls, changed the bed linen, opened the windows, and lit the candles. When all this was done, Johan's father was lifted back into the bed.

"Now I want to be alone with him. I want to lay him out myself," Johan's mother murmured, and she closed the door.

Johan shut his eyes, then opened them again. He looked at Mai, bent over in front of the mirror, the brush running through her hair. From time to time she would count out loud to herself—sixty-eight, sixty-nine, seventy.

Johan wasn't a popular man. He wasn't a man people looked up to. And he wasn't a controversial man. He doubted whether he was a man others would miss. But he was loved. He didn't doubt Mai's love, although he never truly understood why she loved him. When things were going well, he imagined that he was in possession of qualities that he had never dared to reveal, or been capable of revealing, to anyone but her. But when he lay awake at night with his thoughts churning, he imagined that she was the sort of woman who could only love a man weaker then herself, someone who adored her, someone who would always be at her mercy, and that such a love degraded them both. True love was something that existed between kindred spirits, between equals, wasn't it? He looked at her. Never mind, he thought, I'll take a degrading love, if only it's tender as the love between Mai and me.

Once, many years ago, Johan asked Mai to describe herself in six words. He gave her a sheet of paper and asked her to write a list. Johan was a great one for lists.

These are the words she chose:

Strong-willed
Professional
Ugly
Steadfast
Childless
Content
Honest

"You've put down too many words," Johan said, when she handed him the sheet of paper. "You were supposed to write down six words, not seven."

"So what?" she said, and a moment later she'd forgotten the whole thing and moved on to something else. That's how she was. Johan didn't know anyone who did things as quickly as she. It was a question of patience. Mai never had the patience to stick to one thing for any length of time. She walked quickly. Ate quickly. Made love quickly. Tidied up quickly. Thought quickly. Sometimes she snapped at Johan for not doing things just as quickly. For taking his time—to walk, to eat, to make love, to tidy up, and to think.

Later, Johan went over Mai's list. He had asked for six words; she had given him seven. One word had to be deleted.

Strong-willed and *professional*? Yes. She always got her way; she was a reputable and well-respected doctor. The wall of her office was covered with colorful children's drawings. She was forever receiving cards from grateful parents. But she never took her work home with her, as they say. She once told him that she could not remember the names of the children she had treated, not even the ones who had died. Johan found this surprising.

It was a matter of will, she said. She didn't *want* to remember their names. If she had to carry all those names about in her head, the ones who got well and the ones who didn't, she'd never get any peace.

Ugly? No, not ugly. But when Mai used the word she uttered it with something like pride, well knowing that she was magnificent precisely by virtue of her ugliness: her long gray hair, her child's face, and her fabulous big nose. Had she been the slightest bit prettier she would have been far less attractive.

Steadfast? Yes, unfailingly. Mai kept all promises and honored all agreements. It would never occur to her to break a promise, come what may. On one occasion, for instance, she had promised him that they would have dinner at a new restaurant in Oslo that had been getting rave reviews in the press. When they arrived at the restaurant, the maître d' couldn't find their name in his ledger.

"But I reserved a table," Mai told him.

"I'm sorry," the maître d' said, "but I don't have your name. Another evening, perhaps?"

"No," Mai said. "We're dining here this evening."

"But—"

Mai cut him off. "The minute a table becomes available, you let us know!"

Johan and Mai sat down at the bar. It was eight o'clock. When ten o'clock came and they still hadn't been seated, and the maître d' gave no sign that it would soon be their turn, Johan said he'd rather go home and pick up a hot dog on the way.

"No," Mai said.

"What do you mean, 'No'?" Johan said.

"No," Mai said. "We had an agreement, you and I. We agreed to have dinner here tonight. I promised you."

Johan shook his head and sat for another ten minutes. Then he got to his feet and said, "That's it, I've had enough."

Mai remained where she was, staring straight ahead. "I'm waiting here," she said. "I'm waiting right here. I'm having dinner here tonight, no matter what."

So Johan left. Later, Mai told him that she did eventually get a table, close to midnight, and to the chagrin of the staff (the restaurant was getting ready to close) she proceeded to order a four-course dinner, which, to the staff's relief, was nonetheless consumed in record time.

Childless? Yes, but by her own choice. Johan raised his eyes from the sheet of paper. Sometimes, in the bathroom in the morning, after a hot shower, he would breathe softly on the mirror. And a face would reveal itself on the glass, not his face yet one akin to his own. A face he carried with him always. Johan bowed his head over the list once more.

Content, she had written. Definitely, thought Johan. Mai's natural state was quiet, inexplicable, and unassailable contentment. She had a capacity for enjoying what she called "the littlest things in life": a lovely dinner, a glass of chilled white wine, a walk in the forest, Johan's hands, Johan's kisses. Years before, in the first flush of their romance, it used to surprise him how much pleasure she took in his body. She was hungry, passionate, curious, and always eager to make love. As the years went on he realized that all this passion had nothing to do with him. Or, rather, it had less to do with him and more to do with her: her mouth, her throat, her hands, her breasts, and her sex. It all came down to Mai's pleasure in her own body and what her body could achieve when it came into contact with other bodies, what delights were possible.

The last word on Mai's list was *honest*, and Johan knew that this was the word that had to go.

Mai wasn't honest at all. Quite the contrary: she told lies. Pointless little lies that didn't matter, lies never mentioned between them—or, rather, Johan never let on to her that he knew she was lying. Mai was proud, and proud people mustn't be made to see that one has spotted their weaknesses. It's upsetting, like stones thrown at a peacock that, in a moment of great ease, treats you to a display of beautiful feathers.

Letting a coward know that she is, indeed, cowardly can, on the other hand, be very satisfying. Alice, his wife number one, was a coward. "Alice and I were two of a kind," Johan was wont to say. "We tormented each other."

As for Mai's lies: they were of no account. Simply not important.

One evening many years ago, Mai set off on the last train to Göteborg. She had been invited to speak on colic in newborn infants at a conference of Nordic pediatricians. Three days without Mai, Johan thought. The truth was, he couldn't bear being parted from her for so long. When the door slammed behind her, he sat in their apartment in Jacob Aals Gate, rolling a spool of thread around the dining table. It was a Friday evening, and he toyed with the idea of taking himself off to the summer cottage they had bought across the Swedish border in Värmland. Better to be alone in the country than here in town. At least there he had the trees to talk to. He went on fiddling with the spool.

Then he said out loud, to himself, "Mai can sew." And

then he said, even louder, "Alice couldn't sew. Alice couldn't do anything but nag me. And count the pennies. *That* she could do!"

He cast an eye around the empty apartment. He thought he heard laughter from one corner.

"Alice, is that you?" he hissed. "Come back to haunt me, have you?"

He heard the laughter again.

"Bitch!" he muttered.

It was late in the evening. Johan knew that when he started speaking his first wife's name and, worse, when he started talking to her, then desperation lay just around the corner. So he promptly decided that he wouldn't go to the country cottage in Värmland. No. First thing next morning he would travel to Göteborg and surprise Mai.

Surprises are, of course, never a good idea. Johan was against surprises of any sort on principle, and one's principles ought to be taken seriously. It was not a good idea to travel to Göteborg to surprise Mai. For one thing, they never even saw each other and she never found out that he had been there. Never. Not even after he was dead. And like as not she has forgotten all about that seminar. If, on his deathbed, he had asked her, Mai, do you remember seventeen years ago when you took the train to Göteborg to give a lecture on colic in newborn infants? she would have frowned and shaken her head. Mai's memory has never been very good. The best that can be said of Mai's memory is that it is selective. She remembers what she chooses to remember and forgets the rest. Johan believed this was one reason why she seemed so content and secure and why he, an insecure individual, could find peace with her. She simply forgets everything that she does not consider worth remembering.

Johan did not forget. Johan forgot nothing. There were times when he thought that the boil on his face, the bedsores, the bloody incisions, all those things that seeped and ached and throbbed, all those things that were turning his body into a dense swamp, were memories of life lived. That only now, at the end, through pain, had he become a reality.

"Reality is hell," he said.

Only Mai understood what he was saying toward the end, and at the very last not even she could make him out.

He said to her, "You alone could have eased my pain, Mai."

Johan arrived in Göteborg before noon. It was pouring rain. He walked to the hotel, hoping she would still be in her room. He knew she wasn't scheduled to give her lecture until two-thirty and guessed that she would spend the morning preparing. By the time he reached the hotel he was soaked through. His nose, his eyes, his eyebrows were streaming; he could lick the rain off his lips, and it dripped from his coat, the bottoms of his trousers, and his bag. His shoes squished, and his white shirt and his undershorts clung to his skin. He called Mai from a pay phone outside the hotel. The operator put him through, and she answered right away. She sounded happy to hear his voice. Where was he calling from? she asked. Was he at work? Had he slept all right without her beside him? But she didn't give him a chance to answer, just kept talking, told him she was dreading her lecture, worried she'd leave out something important.

Eventually Johan did manage to get a word in. He asked what she was doing.

"Writing, of course," she said. "I'm sitting here writing."

"Yes, I know that. But just at the moment when I called, what were you doing then? I'd like to be able to picture you."

She laughed softly. "At the moment you called, or just before you called, I got up and went into the bathroom to brush my hair."

"A hundred times?"

"No, just a couple of times. I was trying to decide whether I should wear it up or leave it down for this afternoon."

"Leave it down."

"D'you think?"

"Yes."

It felt good, he realized, to be standing like this outside her hotel with the rain drumming on the roof of the phone booth, to be standing in a puddle of water, holding on to the wet receiver, to her voice and the image of her in front of the mirror; the shining hair that he imagined he could see light up the whole of her dark room, the whole of the hotel, the whole of Göteborg.

"What are you wearing?" he asked.

"My stripy nightgown, glasses."

"You mean you're not dressed yet?"

"Well, I got dressed and went down for breakfast; then I came back up to my room and put on my nightgown again. I like working in it. It's nice and loose and not too warm."

"You're warm enough, then," he went on, "in just your nightgown? You've got the window closed so you don't catch a cold?" He gazed up at the hotel and its rows of windows, behind one of which was Mai.

"No," she said, seeming a little surprised by the question. "I've got the window open. The sun's shining. It's really like spring here, just a gentle breeze ruffling my hair. How's the weather in Oslo?"

"It's raining," Johan said.

"Typical," she said.

For a moment or two neither of them said anything.

"What'll it be, then?" Johan asked finally.

"What?"

"Your hair. Up or down?"

"Down, I think." She paused again, then added, "Or maybe up. I don't know."

"I love you," Johan said.

"I love you too," she replied. "Now I'd better hang up and get back to my writing." She sighed. "I don't know how you do it, Johan," she blurted out. "Churning out articles day in, day out, I mean. This, to me, is sheer hell."

"To me too," said Johan, laughing at her. "Don't despair. You'll get there! And tonight you can celebrate."

Then they hung up.

Johan stayed in Göteborg for the rest of the day. He kept an eye out for her, waiting behind a tree until at long last she left the hotel. It was almost two o'clock and still raining. Under her long scarlet raincoat she was wearing a green sweater, a tight-fitting blue skirt, and green rubber boots. Her indoor shoes were probably in the plastic bag she carried in one hand, and her typewritten lecture notes in the bag over her shoulder. She was also clutching a large yellow umbrella on the point of blowing away. Her fair hair hung loose.

He followed her to the convention center and watched as she was swallowed up by the crowd. He decided to wait until her lecture was over, and again he hid behind a tree. Hours went by. There was probably a lot of talk back and forth between her and the other pediatricians, he thought, maybe other lectures. Mai's surely couldn't be the only one. At last she emerged, with two other women. They walked in a huddle like the best of friends, hooting with laughter at the wind threatening to blow them over. Like Mai, the other two were carrying large yellow umbrellas, and it dawned on him that these were furnished by the organizers of the conference. Then he noticed the black lettering: NORDIC PEDIATRICIANS' CONFERENCE 1985.

That evening Mai had dinner in the hotel restaurant with her colleagues. She didn't see Johan, even though he actually stood in the doorway, scanning the restaurant until he located her table. It would never have occurred to her that he could have followed her, that he could actually be there in Göteborg, that he would come all that way. She was deep in conversation with the two women she had joined up with earlier in the day, and to all appearances she was having a terrific time.

When a man's wife goes off to a seminar and then tells lies about it, chances are she's having an affair. But when Johan's wife goes off to a seminar and tells lies about it, she lies about the weather. Johan's wife tells him that the sun is shining and that she is sitting writing by an open window, feeling the spring breeze ruffle her hair.

It crossed his mind that this lie might be a forewarning of a bigger lie, a more pernicious one. The moment Mai said that the sun was shining even as rain was coming down in buckets, he had thought, She's in love with someone else! She's betrayed me! But then he realized that there was no logical connection between the weather in Göteborg and the likelihood of another man in Mai's life. A woman, he concluded, is no less unfaithful in sunshine than in rain.

Johan never did come up with an explanation. It was such a scrappy lie. Neither the truth (that it was raining) nor the lie (that the sun was shining) was malicious, harmful, or even *relevant*. But the fact was, and still is, that Mai tells lies.

Her other lies, when first he became aware of them, were all of the same caliber, if a lie can be said to have a caliber. They were of no account. Johan might not even have noticed them, had it not been for Göteborg.

For instance: Johan and Mai would occasionally call each other at work. If Johan had left home before Mai, he would usually call to ask what she was wearing. It was a kind of a game. She knew he liked to be able to picture her. But more than once he discovered, always by chance, that she was actually wearing something quite different from what she had described over the phone. She might tell him that she was wearing a blue dress when in fact she was wearing red pants. That sort of thing.

But she didn't always lie.

When Mai was thirty-eight, she announced to Johan that she was pregnant but that she'd made up her mind to have an abortion. She had had an amniocentesis, and the test had shown the fetus to be defective. Johan pleaded with her: she couldn't make a decision like this on her own; they ought at least to discuss it, he said. Exactly how far along was she?

"Fourteen weeks," she said, and turned away.

Months later in a bookshop, in the section called "Mother and Child," he found a book with a week-by-week account of pregnancy. He opened it to week fourteen: "The baby's heart pumps twenty-eight liters of blood a day," it said.

Twenty-eight liters of blood.

He saw before him twenty-eight milk cartons.

He saw before him a heart.

But at this particular moment he was standing, staring, speechless, at Mai's back.

"For God's sake, Mai. You never said a word. I had no idea. In any case, it's too late for an abortion. This is a *baby* you're carrying."

"It's not too late."

"It's my baby too," he ventured, and the words didn't even sound hollow to him. I think that in a momentary burst of courage, which deserted him immediately afterward, Johan wanted that child. "You can't just—"

"It's my body," she cut in. "And anyway, it's deformed. We've created this deformed thing, Johan. I don't want to have it. It's a pity, but it's out of the question."

Johan looked at her.

"You're cold, Mai."

"I am *not* cold. Jesus, Johan!"

"What you want to do, it's so . . . lax, morally lax. You can't just—"

"Big words, Johan," she hissed. "Big words. Let's not make speeches about things we don't understand."

She started to cry. For a second she reminded him of Alice, who often resorted to tears in order to bring a discussion to an end.

"I can't stand the thought of going through with this. I can't stand it!" she sobbed. She flopped down onto the floor and ran a hand through her hair. And then she said, softly now, "You couldn't even take care of a healthy child, Johan. You couldn't even take proper care of Andreas. When Alice died he was left all alone in the world. I don't want to bring a child into the world with you, not even a healthy one, and certainly not this sick one."

This was an argument against which, for obvious reasons, he had no defense. A slightly contemptuous smile every time his only son said the word *Pappa*. Mai knew exactly what to say, which buttons to push. His courage deserted him, and he was dumbstruck.

In the middle of the night he would think, *She didn't need to tell me*. She could have said she had to go to the hospital because of some woman's trouble, nothing to worry about, a routine procedure. She could have satisfied him with some such explanation, as easily as saying, The sun is shining; the window is open, there's a spring breeze blowing. After all, she'd already made her decision. She wasn't interested in his objections, his support, his opinion. She was quicker than he, and she had made up her mind.

After the abortion, he went to collect her from the hospital. He said nothing until they were in the car. Then she turned to him and breathed, "I don't want to talk about it. As far as you and I are concerned, this subject is closed."

Johan stared straight ahead and swung the car out onto the road. "Okay," he said.

She kept her eyes fixed on him. He took the road to Majorstua. Would not look at her.

"Do you want to know what it was?" She spoke in little more than a whisper.

"I thought you said you didn't want to talk about it."

"I don't. But do you want to know what it was? I asked, and they told me."

"I'm not sure I want to know that, Mai."

"A girl. It was a girl."

.   .   .

The episode with the baby was never mentioned again. Not the beating heart, nor the twenty-eight liters of blood. And when Mai turned forty he gave her a splendid birthday: breakfast in bed, a picnic lunch in Frognerparken, and dinner in a restaurant. His presents to her were a puppy and a little silver cross she had had her eye on. Johan was not a religious man, but Mai always said that it didn't hurt to believe in something—although she never seemed inclined to expand this vague statement. She wore a long blue cotton dress, and in her hair, which was still fair, she had pinned a yellow rose. She looked like a young girl. The waiter in the restaurant took her for Johan's daughter.

It was only after her hair turned gray—almost overnight, a few years before she turned fifty—that strangers stopped assuming she was Johan's daughter. Johan, on the other hand, looked older than his years.

While sitting in the doctor's waiting room that day, still unaware that his test results were alarming, he made the acquaintance of a little tousle-headed girl. She too was waiting to see the doctor, sitting there with her mother. How old would she have been: five? six? four?

Johan was hopeless at guessing children's ages; he could never even remember how old Andreas was (although he never lost count of how many years it had been since they'd last spoken to each other). The tousle-headed little girl strode across the waiting room, clambered up onto a chair next to him, and in a voice bordering on a shout said, "I hope I never get as old and wrinkly as you."

Her mother looked up from her magazine, chided her

daughter, and apologized profusely to Johan, who dismissed the mother's apologies with a shake of the head. He smiled and asked the little girl, "How old do you think I am?"

The child cocked her head and squinted to show that she was giving the matter serious consideration. She sat that way for a while, staring at Johan until he began to feel uncomfortable. Then she put out her hand, splayed her stubby fingers, their nails adorned by flaking pink polish, and stroked his cheek.

"You're older than my grandpa," the child said, causing her mother to raise her eyes from her magazine, shush her, and apologize again.

"And how old is your grandpa?" Johan asked.

"Eighty-four," she said, "and sharp as a tack. Are you?"

"Am I what?" Johan asked.

"Sharp as a tack?"

"Why, I should say so," Johan replied, speaking a little louder than necessary, "and if you must know, I'm only sixty-nine. Which makes me fifteen years younger than your grandpa!"

He knew he was overreacting, but he was, after all, waiting to see the doctor, who had called and asked him to come right away—which was in itself ominous—and then along comes this tousle-headed child with her decrepit grandpa. Johan was upset, and not only by the little girl's outspokenness and the mother's repeated apologies. At the same time, he wanted to show the mother that he took the child's teasing in good fun. Never let it be said that he couldn't laugh at himself or at a clever little child.

. . .

That same evening as he lay in bed, waiting for Mai to finish brushing her hair, he was searching for the right words. He didn't know how to put it, but he thought, She'll help me. I'm sick, but she'll help me. My life has never been the picture of dignity.

"What is it, Johan?" Pale and frightened, Mai turned to face him. "There's something you're not telling me. What is it?"

"Mai, it's spread. I think it's serious."

There. He'd said it. Mai gave a little gasp. "What did the doctor say?"

"He smelled kind of sweaty."

"Johan!" Her voice was sharp now. "What did the doctor *say*?"

"He said it was alarming."

Mai burst into tears. This time it was no act. She set the hairbrush on the table in front of the mirror, went over to him, and curled up on the bed. Johan stroked her hair.

"You'll have to help me when the time comes," he said.

Mai looked up at him. Her face was blotchy, streaked with tears and snot.

"What do you mean?" Her voice broke. "Of course I'll help you."

Johan went on stroking her hair. He said, "I want to be the one to say when it's over. I don't want to die now. I want to live to be a hundred, just as long as I can be with you. But when I say it's time, I want you to help me."

Mai became very still. She stared at Johan. Then she sat up in bed and slapped his face, the flat of her hand cracking off his left cheek. Johan grabbed her slender wrist and threaded his fingers through hers. She began to cry again.

"Not that!" she whispered. "Not that. Don't ask that of me. I couldn't bring myself to do that for you."

After a long silence, which neither could break, Johan bowed his head. Then he said, "Mai, my life has never been the picture of dignity."

A boil would later erupt on the spot where Mai slapped him. Obviously there was no medical connection between the slap and the eruption, but Johan looked upon the boil as something they had created together. The conjoining of her hand and his cheek had borne fruit; his face had opened up, and he had given birth to a boil. It was a throbbing boil, a repulsive sight. For this reason, for as long as he could, he lay on his side, so that only the unblemished side of his face was visible. One day, though, he forgot himself. When a stray visitor wandered into his hospital room by mistake, he raised his head off the pillow to ask if he could help her. When the woman saw his face, she put her hand to her mouth, yelped something that might have been the word *sorry*, and dashed out of the room.

The boil was a part of him, transforming him, even in his own eyes, into a monster with two heads, one big and one little, that scared other people away. But the boil was also a being in its own right. It had a life of its own. Sometimes it was huge, pulsating and purple as an eggplant; sometimes it was pallid and lackluster. Like a newborn infant, it had to be tended and soothed. It was drained of fluid, smeared with salves, and occasionally even swathed in bandages.

He once claimed to have been woken by the sound of the boil crying.

When Mai ran her fingers over the boil, Johan said, "We made it together, you and I. I carried it. My face opened up and gave it life."

II

THE MIRROR

The surgeons had operated on his body seven times in all. They had taken X-rays and done ultrasound scans. They had examined him, cut him open, and stitched him up again. They had discussed his case and written it up on a chart. Johan Sletten was no stranger. He belonged to them now, to the white coats.

Parked outside the hospital were bicycles fitted with child seats and shopping baskets, hefty chains locked around their wheels. The bicycles testified to the existence of one set of this building's inhabitants: the Healthy, those who left every evening and went home to do the things that healthy people did. For Johan, who was now counted among the others, the hospital had become a home. Once, when he went for a walk in the corridor, a middle-aged woman had stopped him to ask the way to the office of a particular physician. Johan happened to know where this doctor was to be

found and gave the woman precise and elaborate directions. He was a guide. The woman thanked him and hurried
on her way.

While he lived, Johan had three friends: Geir Hernes,
Odd Karlsen, and Ole Torjussen. He often thought of Ole
Torjussen, the one he liked best of the three: journalist,
colleague.

Many years ago, Ole Torjussen fell in love with a young
American woman with dark brown eyes, and in a moment of
heady recklessness he gave up his job at Norway's third
biggest newspaper, left his wife and two children (a boy of
twelve and a girl of fourteen), and moved with the young
woman to New York. They had six months together before
she kicked him out. He flew home to Oslo and his wife, who
took him back for the sake of the children. Freelance assign-
ments offered by his old newspaper made it possible for him
to earn a living. Four years later he would die of leukemia.

Ole Torjussen could tell Johan very little about his six
months in New York. He had been perfectly happy, he said,
right up until the day the girl asked him to leave. And the
happiest moment of all had come one Sunday morning in
May when she had sent him out to buy bread and coffee and
the papers.

The lovers lived in a tiny apartment on West 73rd
Street near Central Park. The girl was studying literature at
New York University and managed on money from home.
Torjussen read books, cooked, kept the apartment tidy, and

managed on money he had stashed away in a bank account of which his wife knew nothing.

This, then, is what happened on the happiest day of Ole Torjussen's life. He came walking out of the shop on the corner where he always bought his bread, coffee, and newspapers. (Yes, always! This shop was part of the order of his new life, like the spot close to Strawberry Fields he took whenever he went to the park to read. Always the same little French place in the Village, too, whenever he had a yen for escargots.) When Ole Torjussen came walking out of the shop on the corner, he was stopped by a tourist—a young man in a T-shirt with white arms and a bag slung over his shoulder, a stranger in the city, no question about it—who asked the way to the nearest subway station.

There were plenty of other people he could have asked, Torjussen said later; the street was awake even early on a Sunday morning. People were on their way to the 77th Street flea market; people were walking their dogs; people like himself were running out for breakfast and the Sunday paper.

But the young man didn't ask anyone else for directions, he asked Ole Torjussen. And Torjussen gave him precise directions, even explaining where he could switch to the express to save time. Ole Torjussen had become a guide in the metropolis of New York. It was nothing, really, but as he walked back to the apartment on 73rd Street with the newspapers under his arm and the bread in a plastic bag and the coffee dripping in a paper sack, he felt as if he had conquered the world.

. . .

Johan had been in the hospital for several weeks when the attending physician on his ward decided that he could go home. Dr. Meyer, who knew Mai slightly from years before, reminded him of a ballet dancer: she spoke with her arms, her hands, her whole body. Every time she uttered a word, moved around doing what doctors do, or stood perfectly still, just listening to him, she seemed to be onstage, dancing. She was beautiful, flat-chested and lightly clad under her white coat. When she came to see him she would perch on the edge of his bed. She was never in a hurry. And one day the following happened.

Dr. Meyer got up from the bed and walked over to the window. Johan could hear piano music. He was about to ask her—Could she hear it too? Was it Tchaikovsky? Something from *Giselle*?—but he couldn't open his mouth, couldn't take his eyes off her as she stood in the light from the window. Suddenly she rose up onto her toes and went into a deep bend from the waist, her body forming a spectacular curve. It was a beautiful, perfect movement. Johan was not quite sure what he was witnessing, but when she finished, he thanked her.

She sat on the edge of his bed again.

"Is it the morphine that makes me think you're always dancing?" he asked. "Is it my imagination?"

"No," she said, straightening his pillow, "it's not your imagination." She made another gesture. "It's time to leave," she said, still smiling, "for a while, at any rate."

He noted those words, *for a while*. The life that went on outside, among the healthy, was no longer his life. But he was to be allowed to mingle with them one last time. The pain had abated somewhat, and his body was responding well to treatment.

"But," said Dr. Meyer, who never showed the slightest sign of dancing when Mai was around, "don't hesitate to call me if anything happens."

Mai took her spindly husband by the hand and led him out of the hospital and into the car, driving straight to the cottage in Värmland. It sat on its own by a lake, just over the border from Norway, surrounded by forest. A peaceful spot.

Johan slept right through that first night, and on the first morning he made love to his wife. His wasted body wound itself round hers until she gently guided his soft penis inside her and moaned.

Even now, when I'm half dead, she manages to take pleasure in me, he thought with wonder.

Afterward, Mai cleaned his boil, drained it of fluid, and tenderly kissed his face.

He so much wanted to savor this time. He wasn't in much pain. It was almost as if he had managed to slip away from the illness. Not that he would have voiced such a thought; he never said, "I've slipped away from my illness." He knew that if he uttered such words, the beast would find him and make him pay. Best to tread softly and try to enjoy life a little. Not too much, just a little. Although even this little bit of enjoyment was not easy to extract, for on their first morning in Värmland, Johan had woken up with a sty on his right eyelid. It stung and itched and suppurated, and his eyelid swelled. Mai had a Swedish colleague write out a prescription for eyedrops. Now they sat, each in his own chair in the living room, Johan inspecting the inflamed spot in Mai's compact. He said, "Do you think it could be anything other than an ordinary sty?"

"No," she said flatly.

Johan blinked again. "The drops aren't doing any good, Mai."

"It'll probably take a day or two."

"But it's stinging even more than it was this morning."

"Johan, it's a perfectly ordinary sty."

Johan opened his eye and felt it throbbing. "You don't suppose it could be anything—you know—serious?"

Mai heaved a sigh. "No, I don't. You've got a sty on your eyelid, that's all."

Johan laughed shortly. "Ever since I was a boy I've been scared of going blind. I don't mean to be dramatic, Mai. I know you think I tend to be dramatic. But I've always been scared of going blind, and this doesn't feel like an ordinary sty to me. It's something more serious. It's definitely something more serious."

Mai tossed her book onto the floor and looked straight at Johan. "You've got a sty, Johan. You're not going to go blind. I can't believe how you can . . ."

She left the sentence unfinished.

"You can't believe how I can . . ."—Johan breathed—
"seeing as I'm going to . . ."

He left this sentence unfinished too.

The next morning the inflamed spot on his right eyelid
was almost gone.

Some days later at breakfast, Johan announced that he
thought they should get a dog. They'd had one before, and
now he had the urge to get another. It wasn't as if he'd given
it much thought. It wasn't even a serious suggestion. He
said it on impulse, out of a longing for a cold, wet dog
muzzle against the tip of his own nose, the smell of a dog's
paws, the warmth and vitality of a dog's body against his
own nervy form. All this prompted him to say, "I think we
should get a dog."

Mai put down the book she had been reading, looked
down at her plate, and fingered a slice of tomato. She didn't
say anything—she merely sighed, once, twice—but Johan
knew exactly what she was thinking: I'm not looking after a
dog on my own.

"Forget it," Johan said. "It was thoughtless of me. The
last thing you need right now is a dog on your hands."

Mai looked at him and smiled.

"What good would a dog be to you, anyway?" he went
on. "You don't even like going for walks." She was still looking at him. "Anyway, you've got me instead," he said. "Woof,
woof."

"Johan, please. . . . Maybe when you're better."

"Woof, woof!"

"Johan. Please. Don't do that. When you're better."

"I'm not going to get better, Mai. For Christ's sake, look at me! I'm not going to get better."

Johan remembered that time a dozen years ago when Mai turned forty—when her hair had still been fair and people were still taking her for his daughter—and he had given her the silver cross and the puppy. To be honest, it was Johan who wanted a puppy—all his life, really—so he gave one to Mai as a present. The puppy was an albino-white Labrador retriever named Charley. Even though the puppy was a bitch, Johan decided to call her Charley; she wouldn't answer to Clara or Kira or Carla or any other name they tried.

Charley was the sort of dog who seemed old as soon as she was past the puppy stage. She was slow and heavy and slightly lame due to a displaced hip, a birth defect undiscovered until she was eighteen months old. When she wasn't ambling through the forest with Johan—she was never nimble enough to run and play with other dogs—she slept in a basket in the hallway, curled up with her big tulip-red nose cradled in her forepaws.

Charley was the most devoted of dogs. Her trust knew no bounds. She greeted everyone with the same affection and gratitude. And one day the following happened.

Charley and Johan were taking a walk around Sogn-svann Pond. Halfway round they came upon a young couple barbecuing by the water's edge. The girl was dressed in a strapless floral-print summer dress, and the young man, who was exceptionally well built and clearly enjoyed showing off his physique, was stripped to the waist. When Charley limped over to him, tempted by the sausage dangling from his fingers, the young man stood up and kicked her. Charley moaned, the way dogs do, and keeled over.

From a little way off, Johan saw the whole thing: the kick, the dog moaning and struggling to get back onto her feet, the muscled young man still dangling a sausage, now with a self-satisfied grin on his face. Johan knew it was time to act. It was the time for Johan Sletten to show the world what he was made of. It was time for him to defend his defenseless dog. Johan should have marched right up to the cruel young man, ripped the sausage from his sausage fingers, and knocked him flat on his back, goddammit! But Johan did no such thing. He took two steps back and hid behind a tree. Johan was no muscleman. Mai called him a string bean, and string beans don't go picking fights with cruel young men. So he took two steps back, hid behind a tree, and called to Charley in a whisper—softly, softly, so as not to give any offense or cause any unpleasantness. Just loud enough for an old dog to catch the sound of her master's voice, get up, and slink off to find him.

It was Charley—good old Charley with her timorous, trusting heart—he was thinking of when he told Mai they should get a dog. Mai said no, and breakfast was ruined. The idyll, the cottage mood, was shattered. Johan got up from the breakfast table and went out into the garden. After a while he went into the bathroom and shut the door. He stood in front of the old mirror over the sink and stared at his face.

He had fixed this bathroom up with his own hands. Blue vinyl wallpaper, blue flooring. The window was open onto the forest and the lake. The weathermen had forecast a fine sunny day, but instead they'd had wind, a little rain, and an unreliable sun—a typical Scandinavian summer sun, which gave no warmth, could disappear behind a cloud any minute—and often did. Johan had been feeling out of sorts all day. He took the uncertain weather personally. Like everything else, the weather was a sign. Pain or the absence of pain was a sign. The books he bought or was given as presents, the books he read, were full of signs. A collection of poems by Dylan Thomas, a gift from his old friend Geir, was a sign. Johan said, "I can fight this. That's what this means. It's a sign from Geir. I can fight this. Mai, do you hear me? *Rage! Rage!* I won't go into that good night. Not gently. No. I don't want to die."

Soon Mai would knock on the bathroom door, and when he did not answer she would cautiously open it and see him there in front of the mirror. She would stand behind him, maybe put her arms around him.

Mai's face was a sign. He caught himself searching Mai's face with something like suspicion, much as a passenger on a plane will search the flight attendant's face when the plane begins to shudder and the cabin lights go out. Is this it? Are we crashing now? Does she look worried? Will it be over soon?

Everything was a sign that might tell him something about his illness. He looked around and asked the sun, the grass, the sky, the books, and Mai, "Am I going to make it through this, or am I going to die?" It was like the time Mai lost—or got rid of, or killed—the fetus; Johan was never quite sure how to think of it, and this was one of the things of which they never spoke. Never. Back then he thought that the change in the weather was a sign. He remembered it as if it were yesterday. The sun had been shining, but then the wind picked up and it started to rain and Mai told him that she was pregnant and intended to have an abortion. He remembered the way the weather suddenly changed. He remembered Mai's face when she told him it was a girl. And he remembered the book he came across in the bookshop with the pictures of a fetus at various stages of development and the heart that pumped twenty-eight liters of blood a day.

In time, however, when Johan's condition worsened, and the pain with it, the signs would cease to appear, cease to be signs, showing themselves to be simply random occurrences. Just as Johan himself was a random occurrence. There would come a time when Johan would realize that the world wasn't trying to tell him anything, that his body was saying nothing, that the pain offered nothing; that the body is flesh and flesh decays. It was simply there—all of it. He had no tacit understanding with the world. Sunshine was sunshine. Rain was rain. Flesh was flesh. Pain was pain. And there would come a time when Johan would clasp his hands and whisper, "Why?" And the answer would make no more sense than the question: "Because."

But now, standing in front of the mirror, he was still hoping something would happen, hoping for a sign, hoping the beast that had taken up residence inside him and cast its shadow over his life would give way to long, unchanging, sunlit days.

My . . . life, he thought. He didn't know what else to call it. He would have liked to have come up with something grand and eloquent, there in front of the mirror. "My . . . life. My life." That was all he could muster. Sip a glass of cold beer. Read. Go fishing. Lie next to Mai, hand in hand, with the scent of her hair and body in his nostrils.

At the same time, listening to his body, he was conscious of a slight headache and a touch of nausea. The nausea frightened him. It didn't take much to scare him into imagining that something nameless, terrible, unthinkable, was about to happen, something he could not foresee and therefore could not guard against or control. Convulsions. Hemorrhaging. Choking fits.

Being hours away from a big, bright, modern hospital worried him. He'd been looking forward to getting away, but now "away" didn't seem a safe place at all. He didn't want to be "away." He wanted to be where it would be technically possible to save his life. Someplace he wouldn't die just like that, with only the trees, the grass, and the still waters of the lake bearing witness. Who would save him if he were suddenly to collapse right now? Mai? She'd barely give him a

Valium if he complained of feeling agitated. She was a doctor, but she lacked access to the necessary facilities and drugs and didn't have the specialist's skills. A man in Johan's condition needed the utmost expertise. He took a deep breath. *A man in my condition needs the utmost expertise.* He stared at the gaunt face in the mirror and held his breath. The nausea was stronger now, a gagging sensation, as if someone had rammed a stick down his throat. Was the headache worse? He went on holding his breath. He didn't want to start retching, because once begun it would go on and on until he was laid out, drained, on the bathroom floor, like a broken twig. Who would save him then?

When Johan was a boy, he and his friends used to have contests to see who could hold his breath the longest. Underwater, in railway tunnels, while someone counted to fifty or seventy or even a hundred. When Andreas was ten, Johan found him shut up inside a wardrobe with a plastic bag over his head. Johan tore off the bag in terrible fear and slapped the boy's face.

"What made you do such a thing, Andreas?"

The boy merely shrugged and walked away.

Once, many years later, he asked Mai, "What is it about suffocation that children find so seductive?"

Mai thought for a moment. Then she put her finger on his windpipe and pressed, then pressed a little harder and kept pressing until he pushed her away.

He exhaled, stared at his face in the mirror, took a step back, and looked himself up and down: the old man's chest; the long, thin fingers; the nails that had not been cut in a while (he must remember to do that first thing, once he was finished here!); the pale, sagging belly, like a kid's white backpack; the legs that had always been spindly. "Hideous cadaver," Johan said out loud. "Hideous, shitty old cadaver," he said, shocked to find himself using the word *shitty*. Such a refined old man! He leaned in closer to the mirror and studied the boil: a fiery red today. It was surely grinning at him.

"Shit! Shit!"

The boil was still grinning. Johan grinned back.

"Shit! Fuck! Cunt! Cock!"

He must have been louder than he realized, because Mai called from the kitchen, "Johan? Is everything okay in there?"

He muttered something in reply.

The voice from the kitchen: "I just popped outside for a moment—"

He cut her off. "Everything's fine, Mai. I'm just cutting my fingernails." He waved his hands about in front of the mirror. "Cutting my fingernails! Cutting my fingernails!"

He could still smell her sex on his fingers. She had tenderly and efficiently slid them back and forth inside herself earlier that morning.

Strictly speaking, thought Johan, death had no business bothering him. He had done all the right things, made his arrangements, struck his bargains, and said his prayers. Other people died, not Johan, although he would never admit to thinking such a thing. He didn't smoke or drink or drive too fast or brag about this clean living, he wasn't the sort to take comfort in other people's funerals, and he wasn't the sort to say, "It won't happen to me." He knew it was exactly this sort of statement that could strike a man down when he least expected it. He took great care never to evince the slightest sign of hubris; the last thing he wanted was to tempt fate. In his relationship with Death, a relationship he had come to regard as a friendship of sorts (not a friendship between equals, to be sure, but a friendship nonetheless), he had been humble, one might even say ingratiating.

"I know it could happen to me. I know you're greater than I. But I'm being good, look at me, I'm being good, and I would be so very, very grateful if you would leave me alone."

When Ole Torjussen returned to Norway after being kicked out of New York by his brown-eyed mistress, his wife forgave him without much of a fuss. Four years later he got sick and died.

"This is what I get for thinking I could find happiness," Torjussen whispered to Johan. "Hubris, that was my downfall."

"Nonsense," Johan told him. But the thought had occurred to him too, and he was relieved to think that he himself had never tempted fate by being untrue to anyone, not even his wife number one, whom he hadn't liked. And he never forgot to give thanks for Mai. Not a single day with Mai was taken for granted.

After Ole Torjussen's funeral, his mourners talked not about his life, nor about his having once "tempted fate" by chasing happiness across the Atlantic. No, what people remarked upon was the deceased's success at dying graciously, peacefully, and speedily. His wife made particular mention of this. The family had gathered around his deathbed, candles had been lit, and Ole Torjussen had professed his love for them all, most especially for his wife. Then he'd squeezed her hand and asked her, yet again, to forgive him.

"For what, my darling?" she had whispered, wishing to hear him grovel one more time.

In his mind's eye Ole Torjussen saw a pair of beautiful brown eyes, an apartment on West 73rd Street in New York, a man giving directions to a stranger who had lost his way.

"For everything!" he whispered, and closed his eyes.

He closed his eyes, thought Johan (who had heard the story of Torjussen's death several times), partly because he was dying and partly to see those beautiful brown eyes one last time.

"He closed his eyes and died with a smile on his face," his wife sniffed.

Johan was just a little boy the first time he appealed to Death. It was on his mother's behalf. She had a cold and a fever, and the boy realized she might actually die and be gone for good. He didn't care about his father, who would in fact die not too many years later, when Johan was fifteen. But his mother! His mother with her beautiful hands, her sweet kisses, her soft round tummy in which he could bury his face. She couldn't die. So he raised his eyes to heaven and promised never again to steal money from his mother's purse, to be a good boy, a nice, obedient boy, if his mother would only be allowed to stay with him. And Death answered his prayers. His mother recovered and everything returned to normal, except that from then on Johan talked often to Death. On behalf of his mother, his sister, and himself. As I say, he didn't care much about his father—not that he told Death that. He told no one. He didn't even permit himself to think such thoughts, since it seemed likely that Death could read his mind. So when his mother recovered, Johan was a good little boy, obedient and nice, even to his father, who was a clumsy, smelly, if well-meaning man. More well meaning than other fathers, always taking the time to talk to Johan and his sister, especially Johan, the youngest. He would read to him in the evening and take him for walks or to the movies, even during the war. They saw the German movie *The Golden State*, filmed in Technicolor, for which Joseph Goebbels himself had written the heroine's last line: *"I did not love my native soil enough, and for that I must die!"* Even this film they saw, despite his mother's protests.

"I'm not seeing it because it's German, goddammit," his father shouted. "I'm seeing it because it's in Technicolor!"

"It makes no difference," his mother hissed. "You just don't get it, do you? It makes no difference. It can be in as many colors as you like, but it'll still be German. People will talk!"

His father had planted himself squarely in front of his mother. As Johan remembered it, as he pictured them there, he saw something he hadn't seen before. He had always recalled his mother as a towering presence and his father as a little man. But now, sixty years on, standing in front of the mirror in the bathroom, he suddenly saw them as they had actually been. His mother had been a tiny little woman. It was his father who had towered over everyone.

Johan's father had planted himself squarely in front of his mother and roared, "Who will talk?"

"They'll all talk!" she shrieked. "All of them! And you know it!"

Johan opened his eyes, and when he caught his own gaze in the bathroom mirror he remembered his parents as he always had and as he preferred to do. She towered and he was little.

Johan's father took his son for walks and to the movies. He was not a bad man but he was, nonetheless, clumsy and smelly (Johan suspected that he didn't wash between his legs properly). What's more, he had no friends as other boys' fathers did. Johan thought his solitude might have had something to do with the war. Other boys' fathers had stories about all the things they had done during the war, and they told them again and again, but Johan's father didn't have a single one. Not a single friend and not a single story.

In 1945, when Johan had just turned thirteen, his mother got sick again. The doctor looked worried when he came out of Johan's mother's room.

Johan walked right up to him and said, "My mamma is going to be okay, isn't she?"

The doctor said one should never give up hope. Johan nodded, silently cursing the doctor for such a stupid answer. He was a doctor, not a minister. Then his father ran a weak, smelly, well-meaning hand through Johan's hair and said exactly the same thing. "We musn't give up hope, Johan. We musn't give up hope that Mamma will pull through this time too."

Johan stared at his father. "No!" he said to himself. "No more!"

He shut himself up in the bedroom he shared with his sister, went down on his knees, and whispered, "Take him instead. Take my father, whom I love, instead of Mamma!"

And it seemed to him that Death whispered back: *But if you love your father as much as your mother, why should I take him when it's her I want?*

Johan considered this. "Because he's lived longer. It's . . . fairer that way."

Everything was quiet for a moment. Johan stared at the ceiling.

Then he heard the voice again. *Are you sure it isn't because you don't really care about your father, Johan? Are you sure it isn't because you think your father is a smelly, spineless little man who might as well die now? Are you sure it isn't because you adore your mother and you'd be lost without her? Is it not the case, my dear boy, that you are asking me to do you a favor?*

"No," Johan replied, clasping his hands. "I love them both. Pappa's a good man; he means well. It just seems fairer for you to take him first. He . . . he . . . he's ten years older than she is."

Johan lifted his face to the bathroom mirror. He looked tired. He *was* tired. There was no escape from this fatigue. He could not sleep, and he was tired; he slept, and he was still tired. It made no difference. He remembered the little girl at the hospital who thought he was as old as her ancient grandpa. This was the face she had seen. Poor child!

The day after thirteen-year-old Johan spoke with Death, his mother got out of bed for a while with a hint of roses in her cheeks. Within a week she was up and about all day, and after three weeks she was well enough to go back to work.

Johan had all but forgotten Death's favor when, more than a year later, he overheard his mother and father talking in the living room. He knew his father had been to see the doctor, but he hadn't given it much thought. Johan heard his father's anxious whispers and his mother's calm, soothing voice. "Everything will be fine. Things always work out fine." Then he heard his father burst into tears, and the words *I'm scared!*

Johan sat up in bed. His father, this well-meaning, friendless little man who had always been good to Johan, was weeping in the living room.

Johan hurriedly clasped his hands. "Thank you, thank you, thank you," he whispered, tears spilling down his face.

He lay down again and shut his eyes. He could still hear the voices in the living room and his father's quiet sobs.

Johan clasped his hands again. "Hey, there!" he whispered in the darkness. "Hey, you!"

No reply.

"I know you can hear me, and I just wanted to say that I'm grateful to you for doing as I asked, but that this is no small sacrifice. I want you to know that. My father's a good man. It's not that I don't care about him. You said I didn't care, but I do."

Johan blew on the mirror. He saw his father's face, the last glimpse of his father's stricken face before his mother closed the door and the howling began.

He didn't want to end up like that. He wanted to decide for himself when it was time, and he didn't want to be a burden to anyone, least of all to Mai, any more than he already was. Mai was seventeen years younger, only fifty-three. And slim, stately, almost beautiful. He tried to summon up Mai's face the way he had his father's, but there was only mist. He could hear her out in the kitchen, humming and clattering dishes and cutlery. It was impossible to picture a face one knew so well. When he thought about it, he realized he seldom saw her face in his dreams. He could envision his mother's face whenever he liked, and his father's as he lay dying, before the blue door was closed, and Alice's face, twisted with scolding, but not Mai's face. If he shut his eyes and worked his way inside to that part of him that continued to burn, he could find the rapture Mai's face awakened in him, not only when they first fell in love but to this day. It was like discovering a clearing in the forest where wild strawberries grew.

Very few who knew him would have described Johan Sletten as a man with an inner flame, but he was aware of a small unaccountable flicker deep inside all the same. At his funeral he was remembered as honest, amiable, witty, intelligent, able. His interest in books, the cinema, and music was mentioned but not overplayed. It would never have occurred to anyone to use the word *passion* in connection with Johan. Not even Mai—when, to many people's surprise, she delivered her husband's eulogy—gave the impression that their twenty-three-year-long marriage had been in any way passionate. Qualities such as friendship, thoughtfulness, understanding, and trust were named. Especially trust—she repeated the word several times.

Now that all this is said and done, it might seem as if Johan was the only one who knew he had an inner flame, a quietly resounding *yes*. Whether or not other people knew it was there, it was what he was prepared to fight for. He would fight as long as he could. It was not impossible to survive this. Johan had made a list of all the stories he had read or heard, about men and women, given much the same diagnosis as he, who had survived. He could be one of them. He wanted to be one of them.

But when he couldn't fight any longer, if it came to that, then he wanted to die with dignity. Before they found him caked with his own shit. Before he became a burden to Mai. She must understand that it would be his choice, his last plea for help. Yes, he would fight, but if and when he found the battle going against him, he would ask for help.

Johan faced himself in the mirror. This thing about a dog, he thought, had left its mark on the day. He didn't even want a dog. When Charley was put to sleep, he'd made up his mind never to have another dog. But a perfectly ordinary conversation between a husband and wife about getting a dog shouldn't have to be so goddamned existential, a matter of life and death like everything else these days. Mai didn't want a dog because she thought that Johan was about to make his exit—now there's drama for you, thought Johan, making a face in the mirror; Mr. Johan Sletten makes his exit—and she didn't want to take care of a dog on her own. Even the most ridiculous, banal conversation revolved around the fact that Johan was about to make his exit. (Although making one's exit really suggests leaving a stage, and he was going to do more than that: he was going to kick the bucket, cash in his chips, pass away, shuffle off this mortal coil.) But talk about it . . . she never would. Not that he wanted to. But they hadn't made plans as they usually did. Mai wouldn't admit that she believed he was going to die, but she wouldn't make plans either. She wouldn't even pretend. That wasn't her way.

The business about the dog had set him thinking, and now he wanted to talk to her. He had wandered around his little Swedish cottage garden, cursing the capricious weather (which he took personally, as a sign), thinking that it was time he took control of the situation. A voice, like another, deeper form of breathing inside him, said that it was high time to take control! And at that moment the sun peeked out from behind the clouds and shone down on him, shone with just a fraction of its enormous power on my spindly friend Johan Sletten.

He turned his face to the sky and let the sun warm him.

It was high time.

Johan did not have much of an appetite at dinner. Food, even good food, nauseated him. But he could still, on occasion, enjoy a glass or two of wine, as he did that evening. Sitting with him at the kitchen table under the blue lamp, Mai remarked, a bit absentmindedly, "Your boil's looking a bit fiery. I'll clean it for you." She stood up.

"Sit down, Mai!"

Mai looked at him, taken aback. She sat down.

"Forget about my face! We need to talk." They both winced at his tone. He took a deep breath. "And there will be no interruptions," he added. He raised his hand to feel his cheek.

"For heaven's sake!" Mai burst out laughing.

But Johan silenced her, saying, "I've . . . I've been thinking."

"I see."

"I want you to hear me out without interrupting. This is important. I need your help, Mai. I need you . . . more than ever."

Mai nodded.

"I'm sick, but I'm going to fight it. You know I want to fight it. I may even recover completely . . . I *may* recover, you know . . . but if not—"

"Johan," Mai interrupted gently, "why don't you just take one day at a time? You're feeling better now, aren't you? Can't we enjoy this time together without thinking too much about it?"

"I want to get certain things sorted out now," Johan

whispered. "So that I can live out the rest of my time with you in peace. That's all I want, Mai, a bit of peace."

"You're not going to get any peace as long as you keep trying to predict the future," Mai retorted. "I could have a heart attack tomorrow, right? Bye-bye, Mai! There's no point looking too far ahead."

"You have to listen to me," Johan pleaded. "I *am* fighting. I don't want to die. But I need you to help me if . . . if my illness should become a burden"—he struggled to find the right words—"a burden to us both."

"You're not a burden."

"But if I become one—"

"I don't think of you that way," she snapped.

"I worry about the pain, Mai."

"Pain can be eased. And I'll be with you. I'll always be right there with you."

He looked at her with gratitude. He said, "I worry about the humiliation. I don't want you to see me like that. I don't want your last memory of me to be the *stink*. I remember when my father . . ." He couldn't finish the sentence.

Mai looked at him and took a breath. "I understand what you're saying, but . . ."

He waited for the rest, but nothing else came. He wanted to know what was supposed to follow that *but*. He wanted to know whether she was going to repeat *I'll be with you*, maybe say *I'll always be right there with you, no matter what*. But she said no more. She began clearing the table. He contemplated her hair, which she had put in a long gray braid, and her big hands with their short, clean nails, a narrow white crescent at the tip of each: a sign of good health, she had once told him. Alice's nails had been flimsy and ragged, and she was always absentmindedly nibbling at them. Sometimes she would have them painted pink. She'd come home and flutter her hands, those teeny Chinese hands, in front of Johan's face and ask him if he thought they were pretty.

He looked at his own unclipped fingernails: narrow white crescents at the tips. Once he had put his palm up to Mai's and said, "We have similar hands, you and I." But she had pulled her hand away, saying it was bad luck to compare them. Mai had promised that she'd be with him always. Hold his hand until it was over. Mai's was the good hand he wanted to be the last thing he sensed in this life. She would take his hand in hers and lead him to the other side.

He had always thought of Mai's hands in this way—as good hands, patient hands. She who was always so quick could suddenly draw her body very close to his. It was the way she stroked him, the lingering progress of her hand across his stomach and down, the fact that it was so slow, so easy and slow. Other women didn't have hands. Only Mai had hands.

Before they went to bed that night, Mai lit a fire. The August summer smacked of fall; the wind was blowing hard, and—after months of long, light-filled evenings—darkness had fallen suddenly and unexpectedly. Johan and Mai sat in their chairs with their books. It might have been any ordinary evening, Johan thought, if not for the nausea, a gob of vomit in his gullet that would not go up or down. And the conversation with Mai that had concluded with the word *but*. Was she going to say that she would be right there with him whatever happened?

"Say it, Mai!" he whispered. "Talk to me!"

He looked at her sitting there in the firelight, her mouth half open over her book, like a little girl with her first detective novel. But Mai is a middle-aged woman, he thought with some satisfaction, even with that girlish aspect. She, too, is mortal, just like all little girls who think they will never die. But the worms will crawl through the locks of little girls too. He smiled and looked at her. It could end here, he thought. Two old friends, Johan and his wife, in their chairs, reading their books in front of the fire on a late-summer evening.

He studied her. The glossy gray braid had grown straggly in the course of the day, sprouting stray hairs in all directions. A pair of round reading glasses perched on her nose, and her face was warm and rosy. He reached out to stroke her cheek but checked himself, reluctant to disturb her.

It could end here. No pain, no howling or fear or degradation. Just this moment—Johan and Mai and the fire in the hearth—and then a long, black night.

Johan shut his eyes and thought of another woman. *Mamma.*

From time to time before she died, they would meet at a coffee shop for muffins and hot chocolate. One day he asked her to tell him about his father. Usually they didn't talk about anything in particular. She would tell him about her insufferable neighbor, the ladies at her bridge club, her long solo expeditions to the old department store downtown. When he asked about his father, she started to say something but stopped abruptly. She looked at him and whispered, "I can't."

Her small lined face turned to his, and her eyes glistened.

"You don't understand. . . . Every time I try to picture Pappa, all that comes to mind are those last days. Pappa covered in . . . Pappa was suffering something terrible, Johan. And there was nothing I could do to help him. It's as if these images have erased all the others, the good ones. There were so many good images. Pappa and I had a good marriage. He was a good man. But all I'm left with are these horrible memories. I can't push them away. I can't wipe them out. I try, but I can't do it."

Johan heard Mai yawning, and soon her book slid onto her lap. The fire had gone out. Neither of them spoke. They simply got on with doing the usual things a husband and wife do every night, without disturbing each other, without getting in the other's way. Turn down the bedcovers. Brush teeth, go to the bathroom, wash hands. Kiss good night. Turn out the light.

But Johan knew he wouldn't sleep that night. He rarely slept now, but he didn't keep Mai awake complaining about it. He had a headache, a dull pain over his right eye, as if some irate little man had driven a fist into his forehead; not that it was unusual to have a headache when the weather was changing so fast. The nausea was worse—it just would not go away—and the comforter was too warm and smelled a little funny, and he couldn't get comfortable. He tried to visualize all the healthy cells in his body smothering the unhealthy ones, the way a psychologist had advised him to do. But instead he found himself visualizing the opposite: death to the healthy cells. He cursed that psychologist, all the rotten psychologists and their rotten advice. He just lay there feeling worse and worse.

"Johan, are you all right?" Mai's voice was soft. She wasn't sleeping after all.

Johan said, "Give me your hand. I'm afraid."

Mai gave him her hand. "Don't be afraid. I love you."

His voice broke. "Will you help me when I can't take it anymore? When it gets to that point, will you help me?"

Mai lay still and gave his hand a squeeze. Neither of them said anything.

For a long time they lay like that, hand in hand in the dark. Johan shut his eyes. He was conscious of her hand and her breathing and her scent and her half sleep, and sleep for him soon seemed possible. His nausea abated, his headache too. Sleep was possible tonight, Johan thought, and he squeezed her hand. Sleep. Peace. You're my best friend, Mai.

And just as sleep was enfolding him in its great black cloak, Mai sat up and switched on the lamp. Johan's eyes snapped open. "What's the matter?" he whispered. "I thought we were sleeping."

"We're not sleeping," she said. "Anyway, I'm not."

"What's the matter, Mai?"

"Johan, what you're asking me to do is against the law!"

"What?" Johan rubbed his eyes.

"What you're asking me to do. What you've asked me several times to do."

"Oh, that," he whispered.

"It's against the law."

"What damn law?"

"Norwegian law. It's against everything the Medical Association of this country stands for, don't you see that?"

Johan was wide awake now. "And what about your own law, Mai?"

She thumped a fist on the comforter and looked at him. "My own law doesn't count, dammit. Do you realize that you're asking me to commit a crime?"

Johan's eyes filled with tears. He hadn't expected this. "Well, we'll just have to go to Holland," he said softly. "Or Belgium, someplace where it's not a crime. And then we'll have to bide our time in some hotel room until this cadaver is rotten enough for you to agree, with the law's blessing—because that's what matters to you, isn't it?—to give me a *legal* injection." He had to stop for breath. Then he said softly, "I thought you wouldn't do it because . . . I thought you had personal reasons. I never thought about the *legal* aspect. I was thinking of this as a personal act, Mai, an agreement between two old friends, an act of mercy, that's all."

"I know," Mai said.

"You're the one who took Charley to the vet to be put to sleep. You didn't balk at that."

"No."

"Woof, woof," he murmured.

She smiled.

"Oh, what the hell," Johan said, as if to put an end to the conversation. "Maybe I'll come through this. That's what I mean to do, you know."

Mai was not listening. She didn't even notice when he tapped her arm.

"Mai?" he whispered. "Where are you? Come back."

She seized his hand. "Would you like to know why this is so difficult for me, Johan?"

"I thought we were sleeping," he said, shaking his head.

There were tears in her eyes. "I think it's monstrous to force a person to go on living against his will. I think it's monstrous that people who are mortally ill and in great pain cannot be given help to die when they choose—if they ask for it, I mean. You talk about dignity. There is no dignity, Johan. People who are dying, old or sick or both, are reduced to helpless infants—first by nature, then by the hospitals. Is that what they mean by respect for human life? I can't see that happen to you. I won't. It goes against everything that is good and beautiful and true."

Johan stared at the comforter. "That's right," he said.

"You ask me to help you, and I will, Johan. I will. You're my husband, and I would give you anything, even this. But I'm afraid. I'm afraid that my courage will fail me because it's you. Because you're my best friend. Because I don't want to see you die, even if life, for you, becomes nothing but pain. And I am scared of the consequences for me."

She's going too far, he thought. I don't want this, not like this.

He said, "Yes, but it might not come to that, Mai. I'm feeling pretty good, actually. I think I'm on the mend."

Mai clasped his hand between her two. She snuggled up close to him and kissed his lips. "My darling Johan."

Johan cleared his throat. "I don't think we should get too carried away, either. Here I am now, lying right next to you, alive and kicking." He got out of bed and started to jump up and down in the white light of the bedside lamps. "See? Alive and kicking!" He waved his arms about as he jumped. "From now on, just call me Jumpin' Johan!"

He was gasping for breath and there was a tightness in his chest, but he went on jumping. He shouted, "Jumpin' Johan jumped and jumped, up and down he jumped." Every time he came down, his feet hit the floor with a thud. Mai put her hands to her face.

"Stop that, please," she whispered. "Come and lie down."

But Johan would not stop. *Thud! Thud!* I'll show her who can still jump till dawn, he thought.

"Look at me!" He gasped. "Look, Mai!"

"Stop it!" she shouted.

"I'll show you who can jump till day breaks and the rooster crows."

She began to cry.

Johan stopped. He was panting heavily. Her face was buried in her hands. He sat down on the bed and stroked her hair.

"Why do you do that?" she shouted.

"What, jumping?" There was a willful note in his voice.

He reached for the tissues they kept on the bedside table, in case he started bleeding during the night, and mopped his brow.

Mai turned to him. "You're the one who wanted to talk about this seriously, so we're talking. But then you have to go and make a joke of the whole thing. Do you know what? You're belittling us, Johan. You're doing everything you can to avoid talking about what has befallen us, befallen both you and me. You're sick. You're not getting better. Do you know how much that hurts? And you refuse to admit it; that hurts too. We need to make plans. We need to make arrangements." Her voice broke.

"I'm going to fight it, Mai." But his voice was faint. Sweat poured off him, however much he mopped, his breathing was labored, and the nausea was coming back. He felt as if some creeping thing in his belly were trying to work its way up and out, but he whispered that he was going to fight this and then he mumbled that she musn't take away what hope he had; she was supposed to take his hand and say that she would be with him, right there with him always. But she did not hear. Possibly he couldn't quite form the words and say them out loud.

Mai said, "Johan, this conversation began with you asking me to help you. I need to know if you are sure you know what you're asking for, and that you're sure this is what you want—if the time comes. That's just one of the things we have to talk about."

"What about the consequences? For you, I mean."

"I don't know."

Mai turned out the light. For a while they just listened to each other breathe.

Johan whispered, "All I want is for you to say that you'll be with me when it becomes hard to bear. That you'll hold my hand. You said that a while back, and I loved hearing you say it. I want to hear you say it again. The other part . . . about you helping me if . . . I hadn't really thought it through properly, and you took me seriously. That scared me." He gave a little laugh. "I don't know what I want, you see. I don't know what will happen, so it's hard to know what I want."

She squeezed his hand; he went on.

"All I want is to lie here next to you."

"And you will lie here next to me."

"That's all. Nothing else."

"That's all."

"Let's forget the other part. I didn't like that conversation. I just want to take one day at a time."

"Then let's forget all about it."

He breathed a sigh of relief.

"Good night, Mai."

"Good night, Johan."

First came the light: white, hot. Then came the headache. Johan was woken by the headache. Or the light. Or both. The sheets were damp with sweat, his and hers. The fist had ground its way deeper into his skull, except that it was no longer a fist, it was a hammer, pounding away. Pounding him to pieces, he thought. "Go right ahead. Don't mind me," he muttered to himself. He dragged himself into the bathroom, threw up in the sink, and stared at himself in the mirror. His boil leered redly. He knew they would have to go back to Oslo right away. It was no use, this being away. He had realized it yesterday, but now there was no time to lose.

He went back to the bedroom. Mai was up. She had turned on the light and started packing.

"I'll just take the essentials," she said, without looking up. "I can come back in a day or so and get the rest, close the place up."

"I think we'd better leave as soon as we can," Johan said.

"I know."

She looked up at him, trying to keep her features composed, but her face told him exactly what she could see in his.

"Is it that bad?" he whispered.

"No, no," she said, turning away.

Johan took her hand and sank down on the edge of the bed. She sat down next to him. They stayed there like that, hand in hand on the edge of the bed.

"I don't want it to be like this, Mai. I don't want it to get any worse. This headache . . . it . . . I don't know why my head should hurt so much."

"We'll get it checked out."

"What we talked about yesterday?"

"Yes."

"I don't know what came over me . . . not to be able to finish a conversation that I actually initiated. It matters so much to me, do you understand? I want you to help me, Mai. I want you to help me when the time comes. I can't take this!" Johan was sobbing now. "Help me, Mai! I need to know that I have some control! Things just keep on happening to me, you know? I need to have some control! Promise me that you'll help me!"

"I will help you!"

"I don't want to be humiliated."

"You won't be humiliated."

"I want to have control."

"You will have control."

"And dignity?"

"And dignity."

"You'll help me?"

"I'll help you."

"You promise?"

"I promise."

She leaned into him, put her arms around him, and whispered, "You're sure about this, Johan? I have to know that you're completely sure."

"Yes."

"You have to tell me if you're not absolutely sure."

"I'm sure."

Johan looked at Mai. She was crying. But there was something else, too, a new look on her face. He had learned to read that face: the grief over the child she had aborted all those years ago, the pointless lies she told that he seldom bothered to comment on; the seconds before she reached orgasm—the way she laughed then—and her mouth when she was asleep, a slack and rather ugly mouth, vulnerable and totally unaware of being observed. Johan looked at that face now.

Her eyes met his. "I think you've made the right decision," she whispered. "No one, certainly not you, should have to suffer more than necessary." She wiped away his tears and her own. "And we have the time that's left to us, Johan. That time is ours."

"That time is ours," he echoed.

She got up and went back to the suitcase. His eyes followed her. She was so light on her feet, like a young girl. And her face, Mai's face. Johan couldn't find the right word. She packed a few things and went out to the kitchen. He heard water running. He sat where he was on the edge of the bed. His head. He wanted to scream: *AHHHHHHHHHH. OHHHHHHHHHHH. AHHHHHHHHH!* Maybe he could sit here and scream until it passed. A blinding white flash. *AHHHHHHHHHHH!* Another flash. He imagined his head, a severed head, Johan's head on a platter. Who was it again? Who chopped off whose head and served it up on a platter? Was it Caesar's head on a platter? No, no, no. Not a hammer, a *sledgehammer*. And Mai? What was it about Mai, about her face? He had always been able to read her face, but this time, before she got up and went to the kitchen and turned on the tap, what was it? A word, he couldn't think of it. She said she would help him. He said he was sure. It was a deal. Then he glimpsed something in her face. It was as if something had finally loosened its grip. He pictured her at the piano on the rare occasions when she forgot that she wasn't gifted enough. What was it her father had said? She wasn't *graced*. On those rare occasions when she forgot she wasn't graced.

Grace, Johan thought. Mai's face. He whispered, "I have no faith. I have no hope. But I do have love."

Could it have been relief?

Again he pictured the look on Mai's face. Yes, that was the word. It was *relief* he had seen in her face when he said he was sure. Not composure, not regret, but relief. Poor Mai.

She had promised to do as he asked. He had begged her, and in the end she had promised, and relief had crossed her face.

Something inside him fell apart. He hadn't thought it would be like this. He wanted to call out to her, shake her, plead with her, only touch her. "This isn't how I thought it would be, Mai!" But he couldn't. It hurt. The words wouldn't come, only sobs. Not even sobs, only weird inhuman sounds that seemed as if they couldn't be his. And the pain in his head, that couldn't be his. Johan stretched out on the bed, pulled the covers over his face, and lay quite still. Like when he was a child, waiting for his mother to find him, take him in her arms, and comfort him until the hurt was gone.

III

THE DOOR

His naked, bluish-white old-man's body is covered by a hospital gown and nothing else. Penis, testicles, buttocks—all on display. Like a grotesque overgrown child in a hand-me-down Sunday dress, he thinks, tugging at the gown. Even with his brain pumped full of the sedative they give you before the anesthetic, he doesn't forget to yank at the gown. Why doesn't the damn thing cover the most vital parts? Johan Sletten, always at pains to keep a certain distance between himself and others, but here he is, flaunting his private parts like some species of sea anemone.

The white coats take no notice of him.

The white coats have no faces, only hands, countless hands, all seeming to belong to one big body. It's like being tended by a giant white octopus, he thinks, but when he opens his mouth to tell them, no words make it out. In a little while the surgeon will have another go at him. He'll cut through layers of skin, fat, cartilage, and muscle, blood running all the while. Although everything is green and cool and quiet here, like the bottom of the ocean. And as the female anesthetist—never a face, just a voice—whispers softly, with infinite tenderness, "Time to go to sleep now, Johan," he sees the small rusty bread knife in its drawer (second from the top) in the kitchen at the cottage in Värmland. He sees Mai, who has just been baking, or is it his mother?

Could it be his mother he sees?

When this is over, he's going to tell the white coats and everyone else down here on the bottom of the ocean about the taste of home-baked bread with butter and freshly mashed wild strawberries with sugar.

Johan's mother was born Agnes Lind. In 1930 she married Henry Sletten, a cautious, well-meaning man. All you could really say about him was that he loved going to the movies, so much that he even went (when that time came) to see German films shot in Technicolor for which Goebbels himself had written the heroine's last lines. Johan's father was a clerk, his mother a secretary. They lived with Johan and his older sister, Anne, in a three-room apartment on Ole Vigs Gate on the west side of Oslo. The children attended Majorstuen school. Life was pretty uneventful. The day peace was declared, Johan heard his mother singing softly to herself in the kitchen:

In my little, little world of flowers,
oh so slowly, slowly pass the happy hours.

The best day of the year, at least as far as the children were concerned and certainly for Johan, the family's youngest member, was Christmas Eve. Even the words themselves—say *Christmas Eve* often enough, and a great green fan seems to unfold, adorned with glittering strokes of color.

Christmas Eve was always celebrated at the house of Johan's Grandmother Lind, a strong-minded gray-haired widow who, despite her stern demeanor and Christmas presents of hand-knitted scarves and woolen stockings, positively adored her family. On Christmas Eve morning, after she set the table with snowy damask, blue porcelain, and the best crystal (with only the odd chip here and there); after she lit the candles on the tree Johan and his sister had trimmed the night before; and after she changed into her nicest red dress—after all the finishing touches, she would take her place by the window, behind the red curtains in her Frogner apartment, with a small glass of sherry in her hand, waiting for her guests to arrive. And when she caught sight of them on the street below, in their winter boots and bulky coats and last year's woolly hats, with brightly wrapped presents under their arms, trudging through wet snow on a bright and beautiful winter evening, she'd whisper to herself, "See, now! Here comes my little family!"

Johan gasped. How it all came back to him! He hadn't

even opened his eyes, and it all came rushing back: Christmas Eve. Granny. And Mamma.

Until her dying day, Johan's mother tended her own little, little world. He could hear her voice far away, beyond the door. Not the bedroom door, blue and closed, his father's door to heaven, but the kitchen door, which by no stretch of the imagination could have been said to be improper—or anything else, for that matter, except safe—because it was always ajar. Beyond the kitchen door, a glimpse of his mother's hair, the sound of his mother's voice.

The cannula inserted into his hand didn't hurt; the sheets were stiff, clean, white, boiled in one of those big one-eyed washing machines down in the hospital basement. The white coats came and went. His body was no secret to them. They had opened him up, looked inside, helped themselves to this organ and that, laid hands on everything that beat and breathed and lived. But they hadn't touched the beast. Maybe they had taken a little bit here, a little bit there. But the beast, no, not the rat. It was a rat that had taken up residence inside him, dancing, whistling, mating, and pressing out new rats right under the white coats' noses.

They would soon be moving him out of intensive care and back to the ward with the other patients. Mai had already been to see him. When he came to, she was there, holding his hand and stroking his cheek. After a while, when she was confident that he was fully conscious, she whispered to him that they hadn't been able to do anything.

The white coats had opened him up, looked inside, and concluded that there was nothing they could do. Nothing but stitch him up again.

"Do you understand what I'm saying to you, Johan?" she whispered.

"I think so."

"I wanted to tell you myself. I wanted . . ."

Johan nodded and looked up at her. "Did you know, Mai darling, that Pappa painted the bedroom door blue? He said it was a door to heaven."

Mai leaned over him and kissed his lips. He caught the scent of her long hair. Apples, or possibly pears. Fruit of some kind, anyway.

Later they wheeled him along to a ward with six beds. There was only one other patient, a man who kept coughing. Johan asked for a screen. A screen was provided. He didn't need to ask for a morphine pump. That too was provided.

This was in the middle of August. Three weeks later he was dead.

It came as no surprise to anyone. He might have survived for another month, maybe two, who knows? But the beast would have triumphed in the end, and the pain might have been bearable or it might not.

Mai, at any rate, deems Johan's pain no longer bearable. One evening she comes and sits on the edge of his bed.

"Johan," she whispers. But he does not answer, just moans faintly. She looks at him for a good long while before opening her purse and taking out two syringes. She has come prepared. She had to. She cannot take the risk of anyone coming in and disturbing her, possibly kicking up a fuss, or of having her courage desert her, once she starts fiddling with vials and syringes.

"Johan," she says again.

He opens his eyes and looks at her, looks right at her.

"It's time . . . isn't it?" she asks.

And he looks at her.

"I think it's time, Johan." This time she isn't asking.

He says nothing. But she knows him. They have a language all their own. He'd said so himself, many times. Or was it she who had said it? Anyway, it is time.

"I love you," she whispers, and he closes his eyes.

Now she lifts his hand, moistens the skin of his upper arm with a wad of cotton, and injects him with the barbiturate. She sees that he is sleeping and that he feels no pain; that it is good. So she gives him the lethal injection. She watches and waits. So quick and yet so imperceptible. No change in his facial expression, just a trickle of blood from the boil on his cheek. Not much. What had she expected? She's seen people die before. It's like exhaling. She lifts his wrist and feels for a pulse. It's almost over. She bends down to him, her blouse rustling. She puts her ear to his chest. Good. It is done. She steps back.

Three weeks earlier, Johan shut his eyes and thought that Mai's hair smelled nice. He pictured her standing in front of the mirror, running the brush through her hair, one-two-three-four-five. . . .

If he were to sit up in bed, if he could just manage to sit up, he would catch a glimpse of Mamma's hair beyond the kitchen door. He would hear her voice. The songs she used to sing. One song especially, that silly little song she loved to sing long after everyone else had forgotten it:

> *Among the dreams so fair*
> *That in my heart I hold*
> *Is a vision of joy so rare*
> *that e'er will linger there.*
> *In my little, little world of flowers . . .*

"Do you remember our walks, Mamma?"

"Yes, of course I do."

She sat down on the edge of his bed, gazing at him with a worried look, the way she did when he was small and running a temperature and had to stay home from school. She wore a blue dress and beige walking shoes. Her long dark braid hung down her back.

"Would you put your hand on my forehead, please, Mamma?"

He couldn't have been more than six or seven that summer, so it must have been 1939. The family had rented a house in the country, and every single day Johan and his mother went for a walk to look for wild strawberries. She walked ahead and he followed behind, each carrying a white pail, Mamma with her long brown braid, her thin white cotton dress, and her bottom lurching from side to side as she walked.

"You had a long brown braid and a thin white dress," Johan said out loud.

When he looked up, she was still sitting on the edge of his bed, smiling.

"But one day we went our different ways," Johan said.

Little Johan spied a clearing in the forest and wandered off, away from the path, away from his mother. There in the clearing, among the moss and twigs, under a big tree, he found the wild strawberries. His eye fell first on one big red berry, and another, then yet another, and when he bent down for a closer look he saw that there were lots of them. Lots and lots, enough to fill a whole pail.

Johan turned to look for his mother. He wanted to show her.

It was always his mother who found the strawberry patches, never Johan, until today. And every time his mother found a patch she'd beckon to him and put a finger to her lips, warning him to be very quiet. As if the strawberries would turn into clover and moss before your very eyes at the first loud sound or sudden movement. You hardly dared blink.

"Patches like this don't really exist," she'd whisper. "It's best to pick them before they disappear. Don't take your eyes off them."

He knelt down on the mossy ground and picked and picked, turning every now and then to look for her. Where was she? He didn't dare call out to her until the pail was full.

Here he was, little Johan, picking enough berries for the whole family. She'd be so proud of him!

But why didn't she come? How could she not tell that he had found such a patch, such a place, the sort of place where you had to be quieter than quiet, or else it would all disappear? You had to trick the place into thinking that you hadn't seen it, hadn't touched it, that you weren't there at all. So Johan picked and picked, but with each berry he dropped into his pail he turned to look for his mother (even calling out to her once, very softly, because the place could hear everything), and each time he reached to gather more—yes, even more—he expected the place to exact its revenge, to turn into a heaving, gray, monstrous swamp.

Finally he shouted, *Mamma! Where are you?* He looked around: the trees, the sky, the grass. Nothing. Now he really had ruined everything, and his mother hadn't even heard him. Everything was ruined. Now it was only a matter of time. He lay on the mossy ground, hands over his ears, thinking that the heaving gray swamp was bound to be a lot more dangerous than the monsters. *Mamma!*

And then her fingers were in his hair, her voice high above among the treetops and the light. "Johan! What's the matter? I've been right over here the whole time."

He rolled over onto his back and gazed at her: still in white, smiling, and with her index finger to her lips.

He sat up. "Mamma, look!" he whispered.

He showed her all the berries he had picked before he got scared. She smiled, bent down over the pail, put her whole face inside it, and inhaled their scent.

"You get to carry them all home." She smiled. "They're all yours, every last one."

When Johan opened his eyes and looked around, it was evening. Hardly a sound to be heard, only his neighbor coughing on the other side of the screen. He didn't know anything about his neighbor. Sometimes, when he was alone, he wondered whether he ought to ask. Introduce himself or something. Sometimes this loneliness was almost too much to bear.

But he could not find the words. There was no way he could just come out with it, he thought. There was no way he could call out to this complete stranger coughing in the next bed, Hello, my name is Johan Sletten, and this loneliness is almost too much to bear.

Mai came to see him daily. At first, after what was termed the last, and unsuccessful, operation, they didn't say much. She held his hand, asked him if his wound hurt, and moistened his lips for him. After a while, he began to babble. The morphine was a blessing, a veritable gift from the gods. Named after Morpheus, the god of dreams, son of Hypnos, the god of sleep. Some days he didn't feel the least bit sleepy, and the morphine seemed to perk him up. One day when Mai arrived he was sitting in bed, propped up on pillows and reading a biography that had just received a good review in the paper.

Mai perched on his bed. She was wearing makeup. Not a lot, just a touch on her lips and eyes. Mai never wore makeup, but she was wearing it now. It looked pretty.

She also wore a red silk scarf wrapped around her head. Against the long gray hair it made her look rather artistic, he decided. Kind of Karen Blixen–ish. He told her as much.

"And when you write *my* biography, you'll call it *Dance in the Vale of Morphine*," he said.

"*Dance in the Vale of Morphine.*" She laughed.

"That's right. It will be a long and impassioned elegy on my life. A title like that will endow both you, the biographer, and me, your subject, with a sort of mysterious aura of degradation."

"Degradation, indeed," she said.

"Yes, Mai, degradation. Give the impression that I lived a hectic, reckless, ruinous life."

Mai stroked his cheek. "But you're still my Johan."

There it was again, that gentle voice. *Ah, but you're still my Johan.*

He pushed her hand away, startling her. Her eyes glistened, but he refused to look at her. The man in the next bed coughed.

Johan muttered, "You're wearing makeup, Mai."

"No, not really. I just—"

"You put on makeup for me. You wanted to look especially nice when you came to the hospital to visit your dying husband."

"I always wear a little makeup. You know that. Today's no different."

"You've got a red scarf in your hair too."

"Yes."

"You look very nice."

"Thank you."

She lowered her eyes. They were still red. Then she said, "I spoke to Andreas. I asked him to come to the hospital."

"I see. What did he say?"

"I told him that maybe it was time."

"So you think he might come?"

"He told me he's living with someone."

"Finally! How old is he?"

"He's over forty. Forty-three, I think."

"Over forty, eh?"

"He said he's living with someone. Her name is Ellen."

"Ellen," Johan repeated. "Is she over forty too?"

"No, no. Not at all. Twenty-four, he said. And a lovely girl, I gather. She works in production."

"Production of what?"

"I've no idea," Mai said. "Production. That's all he said: *production.*"

"Oh, for goodness' sake, Mai. I mean, the first thing you ask is, 'Production of what?'"

Mai sighed. He turned to look at her. She bit her lip demonstratively. "Johan," she said, firmly now. "You haven't spoken to Andreas in eight years. And I barely know him. I thought it would be a good idea if you two had a chance to talk before . . . well . . ."

Johan turned toward the screen. "Did you hear that?" he

called to the stranger on the other side. "I've got a son! His name's Andreas!"

The stranger coughed. Johan could make out a shadow stirring on the other side of the screen.

"And he's living with someone, a real dish, only twenty-four. He's over forty himself."

The stranger heaved a sigh. "Aw, shut up! I've got a son, too, you know!"

Johan started and leaned closer to the screen, straining to catch anything else that might be said. But there was nothing else, only the sound of a body endeavoring, with some difficulty, to turn from one side to the other in a high hospital bed.

He turned back to Mai. Her eye makeup was smudged now. Johan grinned sheepishly and gave her his hand.

"Tell me what Andreas said. Does he want to see me?"

"Yes, he came around to it in the end. I had to hint that it was . . . that you had . . . that there might not be very much time."

He gaped at her and bolted upright in bed. A jolt—as if his stitches had just burst. He bellowed, "Why the hell did you do that?" Mai opened her mouth to explain, but he wasn't finished. "Why did you *hint* at anything at all?"

"Because Andreas is your son. He has a right to know. This is a chance for you two to make your peace with each other. I'd really like you to make your peace before it's too late."

"For God's sake, Mai. The way you talk, anyone would think I was going to be done for tomorrow."

"I'm talking about reconciliation. All I'm saying is that this is a time for reconciliation." She thought for a moment. "Johan, I said as much as I did to Andreas because he told me that Ellen is pregnant."

"Who the hell is Ellen?"

"His girlfriend. The girl I told you about."

"The twenty-four-year-old?"

"Yes."

Johan guffawed. "The one in production!"

"Yes."

They both fell silent. Then Mai said, "A grandchild, Johan. She's nine months along. The baby's due any day now. That's why I felt I had to tell Andreas as much as I did."

Evening came again. Mai had left long before. Then came night. Why, he wondered, did she have a red silk scarf in her hair?

"She's sprucing herself up, Johan."

It was Alice's voice.

Alice, wife number one, the Horse, alighted on his bed.

Johan sighed. It wasn't fair. Wasn't he suffering enough as it was? He wanted to ask the man on the other side of the screen whether he too received visits from the dead. It was, he would say, as if the walls between this world and the next were starting to dissolve. But he decided against it. In order to talk to the man behind the screen he would have to turn around, and even the most simple movement was terribly painful, not worth the effort. So he lay where he was, eyes wide-open. He tried to think of Mai but found no escape there. So he faced the fact that Alice was sitting on his bed, looking the same as ever.

"You haven't changed, Alice."

She looked him up and down. "I can't say the same of you, Johan. You look awful."

"It's always a pleasure to hear your voice. I've missed you."

"I haven't missed you."

"No. No, I didn't really think you would. Who are you nagging now, Alice? The Almighty, perhaps?"

She made no reply.

Johan went on. "Our son's going to be a father. Did you know that?"

"I knew."

"High time, if you ask me. He's over forty."

"He's forty-three."

Johan took her in: her hands, her fingers with their bitten nails, her horsey face. Of all the ghosts who might have visited his bedside, why her? Why not his old friend, the late lamented Ole Torjussen? Why not someone famous—Joe Louis, for example; maybe Strindberg?

She interrupted his musings, whispering, "Are you leaving him anything, Johan?"

"What the hell?"

She inspected her nails. "No need to get upset. I just want to be sure the money will go to Andreas. I don't want money that was, strictly speaking, *mine* going to your new wife. I inherited it. It was *my* father's money."

"It's in the bank, Alice. I haven't touched it."

"One hundred fifty thousand kroner, plus twenty years' interest?"

"Something like that, yes."

"That's a lot of money."

"It will all go to Andreas. I promise."

"I don't trust you."

"You never did."

"And with good reason."

Johan groaned. "Alice, you're no longer with us!" He propped himself up on his elbows and screamed, "You're no longer with us! You've been dead for twenty-five years! Surely you didn't come all the way from your world to mine to argue about money! Even *you* aren't that petty!"

She said, "You are, for all intents and purposes, in *my* world now, Johan."

"Go away!"

She pouted. "Poor little Johan."

He mimicked her voice. "Poor little Johan! Poor little Johan!" Tears welled up and he hurled a pillow at the wall. "Go away, I said! Go away! Leave me alone!"

"Johan, my darling. No need to make a scene." She peered at him, leaned closer, and whispered, "What's that you've got on your cheek, a boil? Looks pretty gruesome. As if there were two of you."

"Why can't you leave me alone?"

"Do you remember saying that if I went to heaven you'd

rather go to hell? So we wouldn't have to spend eternity together?"

Johan nodded. "Did you get to heaven?" he asked.

"It isn't anything like that," Alice said. "No heaven, no hell. Just death, or something worse."

Johan hummed:

Maybe death he lies a-lurking ahint some ragged coral reef—
He may be hard, but he is fair, so sing hey, sing ho.

The man behind the screen coughed. No one else was in the room. Where was Mai? Why didn't Mai come? What time was it? Johan was about to turn over and say something to the coughing man, but then he heard Alice's voice again: ranting, grating, whining, droning on and on.

"Why did you push me into the water, Johan? You knew I couldn't swim." Alice fixed him with her gimlet eye. "Why?"

Johan pondered the question. At last he said, "I don't know. It just seemed like the thing to do. You were standing on the edge of the dock, and it struck me that you had to go in."

By midmorning, when Mai arrived, Johan felt better. He was sitting up, having finally managed to catch some sleep around daybreak.

She wore a dress he hadn't seen before: tight across the bosom and waist, flaring out from the hips. A lovely red dress, although possibly a little on the young side for her. She was over fifty, after all.

"New dress, Mai?"

"No," she said, settling herself on his bed. She fiddled with a sleeve and laughed at him. "I found it in the attic."

"We don't have an attic!" Johan protested. "There isn't even an attic in our building."

"You know what I mean. In one of those old trunks in the storeroom in the basement."

"I see. So that's what you meant."

She looked down. "I spoke to Andreas again. He'd like to come see you. Are you up to it?"

"Yes." Johan stared at her. The earrings were new too, red stars dangling from silver threads. "You mentioned reconciliation," he said.

"Yes."

"He'll inherit everything, you know, Mai, one hundred fifty thousand kroner plus twenty years' interest. It was Alice's money. I can't leave you anything except debts."

She looked at him and stroked his cheek. "Did you have a bad night, Johan, my love? You look tired. You're having a hard time of it, aren't you?"

He knocked her hand away. "I had a very good night. I feel fit enough to run a marathon. Do you have any idea what kind of a man Andreas is?"

"You know I don't really know him that well. He seemed nice enough on the phone this time around."

"He's unbearable. He's the kind of person who always has to set people straight: friends or strangers, young or old, everybody! He has no qualms whatsoever. Say, for example, that somebody mispronounces a word. Andreas will purse his thin little lips and promptly correct him. The problem is that, almost without exception, *he's* the one who's wrong."

"Oh, dear," said Mai.

"He was in a restaurant once with some new friends," Johan continued. "Take note of that, Mai. Always *new* friends. There is no one on earth Andreas can point to and say, That's my *old* friend so-and-so; we were at school together . . . no one—"

"You don't know that, Johan," Mai interrupted. "You haven't seen him for eight years."

"He's my son. I know." Johan took a deep breath. "Anyway! He was in a restaurant with these new friends, and one young man announced that he was going to have *chèvre*. Whereupon my son smiled and said, 'It's *chevré*, with the stress on the final *e*. And an *accent aigu*. So.' He pursed his lips and raised his hand slightly. '*Chevré!* Simple, right?' No one told him he was making a complete fool of himself with his absurd French pronunciation. They just let him ramble on, indulged him, and seemed to hang on his words. They asked whether he spoke French, and Andreas said, Oh, yes, he spoke a little. Not much, but *oui, oui*, absolutely. In that case, had he perhaps read the works of Marcel Bavian, a much underrated French writer whose short stories were enjoying something of a revival? It was a young woman who asked the question. And naturally Andreas had read Marcel Bavian. Loved his work, especially his short stories. In fact, he said, Marcel Bavian wrote the most perfect short stories:

spare, yet rich, devoid of literary pretension, and aimed straight at the reader's solar plexus."

Johan looked at Mai.

"That's the kind of man he is. Not until later does it dawn on him that when they laugh, they are laughing at him."

"But how do you know all this?" Mai was smiling. She was caught up in the conversation. They were chatting; he liked that.

"He told me about it, but not quite the way I just told you. Oh, no! Triumphantly, Mai! Telling me how he taught this charming new friend of his how to pronounce the name of a French cheese . . . and asking whether in all my years as a critic I had ever come across a writer by the name of Marcel Bavian. Had he been translated into Norwegian, by any chance? No? *Really?* Too bad."

Mai lowered her eyes. "He might have changed," she said. "That was a long time ago."

"Do you think people can change, Mai?" He remembered his last day at the newspaper, face-to-face with Dolores, the gorgeous summer intern. The looks. The sniggers. The degradation.

"I don't know," Mai replied. "I think so. I've changed."

"Have I changed?"

Mai looked at him, her eyes on his face. And in her eyes he could read where things stood with him. He asked her for a mirror, and she produced a compact from her purse.

The first thing he saw was his waxen skin. And then the boil, intent on devouring his whole cheek. Finally the familiar wryness, the result of his plucking one eyebrow bald and leaving the other bushy.

He said, "I don't know what you see in me. I'm old and ugly and I'll be dead soon."

"But you're still my Johan, and I love you."

Her voice was soft and persuasive. Still looking at himself, he laid his head on her shoulder. *Maj from Malö*, he hummed, *bonny Maj, you whom all the waves long to kiss.* She stroked his face and gently took the mirror from his fingers. She drew closer to him and whispered, "You're in pain, I can tell."

The time had come for a conversation of another sort. He could tell by the sound of her voice: *You're in pain, I can tell.* He wasn't up to it. He would really rather not.

He said, "Yes. It does hurt sometimes. It hurts to turn over in bed at night. And my head . . . this headache. But I don't feel so nauseated now. So that's a good thing."

"I spoke to the attending physician. Emma Meyer."

"The dancer."

Mai looked at him blankly. "What are you talking about?"

"Oh, forget it."

"Anyway, Emma says—"

"Emma?" Johan interjected. He hated this bandying about of first names. Emma! He didn't like the idea of a physician who was making decisions regarding his life being called something as . . . as *literary* as Emma and—particularly—being in some way a friend of Mai's.

Mai corrected herself. "Dr. Meyer says the last tests show the reason for your headache."

She didn't need to say any more.

"I thought the headache was caused by the changing weather. It's been so hot and humid," Johan remarked flatly. "And I'm feeling a little better now. My head doesn't hurt as much as it did last week."

"No," Mai said quietly.

"So, as I say, I thought it had something to do with the weather or the strain of the last few weeks, a psychological reaction of some sort. Headaches can be stress-related, everybody knows that. Even children have headaches brought on by stress these days. I was just reading an article about it in the paper. They catch stress from their parents. It's a big problem."

Mai nodded.

"But what you're saying is that Dr. Meyer's tests have shown something else," Johan said, looking her in the face.

"I wanted to tell you myself," Mai said. "I thought you'd want to hear it from me."

"I would actually have preferred to hear it firsthand from a doctor," Johan snapped.

"I *am* a doctor!" Now it was Mai's turn to snap.

Johan lowered his eyes. Didn't it count for anything that he fought every day? Sometimes he actually came close to giving up, but other times . . . at other times he looked around him and could say to himself: *This day too I am here. It grows light in the morning and dark in the evening, and I am here in that light and in that darkness.* Didn't that count for anything? That it grew light in the morning and dark in the evening; that he repeated these words to himself like an incantation, as proof . . . but of what? He wasn't quite sure. Still, it calmed him to say it again and again. Say it a thousand times. Say: *It grows light in the morning and dark in the evening*. But did that count for anything with the others? With Mai? With the white coats?

They took pictures of his body, imaged his innermost recesses, slid him into machines with eyes that could see straight through him—they were treacherous, those eyes. They scanned his organs one by one and decided that the problem lay there and there and there. And this *there and there and there* told them all they needed to know about Johan Sletten.

He looked at Mai. "Am I going to lose control?"

"Johan—"

"Goddammit, Mai, am I going to lose control?"

She did not answer. Instead, she looked at the floor. She closed her eyes and rubbed her temples.

"I don't want . . . I don't want to become . . . a vegetable." He raised his voice. "You've got to do something, Mai!" he pleaded. "Do something!"

"I think you're right," she said. "You should be talking to Dr. Meyer about this, not to me. I shouldn't have said anything."

She would not look at him, even though he was staring right at her. Was it because she knew that when he looked at her it was like looking in a mirror? Was it because she knew that every expression, every gesture, every glance betrayed not only what had passed between Dr. Meyer and herself but also the conclusion to which they had come? There was no way back. It was all over. The worst had happened. And after the worst—nothing. His head spun; he felt his chest pounding, the nausea rising. He started to cry, and Mai put her arms around him.

"Is it going to change me? . . . Am I going to lose control?"

Mai still did not look at him. She said, "Everyone is going to be doing their very best for you."

"I'm doing my best, too," Johan sobbed. He grasped her hand. "I'm doing my best, don't you see that?"

Mai ran a hand through his hair and whispered, "I see that, Johan. I do see that." She caught her breath and hesitated for a moment. "And when you feel you can't fight it any longer, don't worry; you won't have to."

"No?"

"No."

"You promise?"

"I promise. But I need to know that you still want me to keep the promise you asked me to make in Värmland."

Johan pulled away and dried his face with a corner of his pillow. "I don't want to talk about that right now!" he said. "For God's sake, Mai! Don't push me!"

But she persisted. "I don't mean to push you. Johan, darling. I don't want . . . It's just that you *might* lose"—she struggled to find the right words—"you might suddenly . . . suddenly no longer be capable of making decisions."

"And then what?" Johan cried.

"I'll abide by your wishes," she whispered.

Mai got to her feet. Her red dress was made of some heavy material. It looked expensive, and it suited her. She looked beautiful today but tired, too, very tired.

All at once he realized that for her it was over already. The decision had been made. They had agreed that she would help him when it became too much to bear, and now she was waiting for it to become too much to bear. He wasn't ready. He could still say yes! *It grows light in the morning and dark in the evening.* And in those words there was dignity. Not for her—for her it was day after day of pointless waiting. Only afterward, after his death, would she be able to fill her days with purpose again, with tears and memories and comfort and reconciliation. With life. His death would be—again he saw Mai's face at the moment she made the promise—his death would come as a relief.

Johan closed his eyes.

Mai's face reminded him of something. This was not so surprising; memories kept rushing back now, like children demanding attention. Sharp, detailed images but also sounds and scents and sensations. A white neck. A voice. An index finger. A lock of hair. He wished he had the strength to write it all down so something would be left behind. Something of himself, something that could not be misunderstood. And now, picturing Mai's face at Värmland when she had finally made her promise to him, he was reminded of the time he sat between his mother and his sister on the sofa, with his father howling on the bed behind the closed blue door. He remembered their hands over his ears, then their hands coming off.

The sound then: deep breathing. Nothing but the sound of his mother's and sister's deep breathing. As if they had been underwater, and only when his father drew his last breath could they shoot to the surface and fill their lungs with air.

He looked at Mai. Her weary face, her lips, her eyes, her earlobes, the red stars dangling from silver threads. He opened his mouth to say something but stopped himself. The promise she had made him in Värmland. Or the promise he had made her? He was no longer sure. At any rate, they had an agreement. Didn't he owe it to her to get it over with? For her this was not time, simply waiting. It might drag on for weeks, months even. One thing for the dying, quite another for the living to bear. The not knowing how long, that was the unbearable part. The remorseless part. Even though—do you hear me, Mai?—even though it grows light in the morning and dark in the evening.

How much time had passed since that conversation in Värmland? Days? Weeks? He'd lost count.

Johan stared at his bedside table. These were his things: a morphine pump, an almanac, a passable novel by an American woman Mai admired—but why on earth, he asked himself, was he forcing himself to read a page a day of this passable novel? This wretched novel that only Mai and women like Mai (it crossed his mind to wonder exactly what kind of women these were, but he did not pursue the thought) would enjoy? In all likelihood it was the last novel he would ever read, and it was only half good or half bad, which boiled down to the same thing: totally worthless. His last novel. You'd think he would have hurled it to the floor, ripped it apart, jumped up and down on it, spat on it, screamed—yes, *screamed*—it to death. How dare such a thing lie there on his bedside table presuming to be the last novel of his life? This was a time for masterpieces. This was a time he should immerse himself in the one book he could not die without having read, the first, last, and only great work. Johan breathed deep, considering. *Macbeth*, perhaps? Or *The Sound and the Fury*? *War and Peace*?

Again his eyes fell on the bedside table. Other things: a comb, a handkerchief, a watch, a Discman, a Walkman. Two CDs and one tape of consequence: Mozart's *The Magic Flute* and Bach's chorales on the CDs, an amateur recording of some of Schumann's songs on the tape. Songs, but no one singing, just Mai playing. Johan recalled a conversation with Mai, a snippet of a conversation, actually. Nothing she was likely to remember herself. It was something she had told him about Robert Schumann, something he had not been able to get out of his head. How during a trip to Holland in 1854, Schumann fell ill and had to return home, where he was committed to an asylum, having totally succumbed not only to syphilis but also to the music—glorious, tumultuous, devastating music—that rang in his ears wherever he went. "All clamor and noise is transformed in his head into music. He says it is a music so magnificent, played by instruments so wonderful, that its like has never been heard on this earth . . . Robert suffers most horribly," Clara wrote in her diary. Either Clara had been advised not to see her husband, or else she did not want to see him. And that was how Schumann spent the last two years of his life: in an asylum in Endenich, near Bonn. His only visitors were Johannes Brahms and his friend Joseph Joachim.

Spiteful tongues accused Clara of heartlessness, for not being by her husband's side when he needed her most.

"But I wouldn't have gone either!" Mai had exclaimed. "Why should she go to see him? It would cause nothing but pain." And then she had said something Johan had never forgotten: "Schumann wasn't Schumann anymore!" What exactly did she mean by that? What do you mean, Mai? Johan had never asked, not then, not now. They were only words she had blurted out over a glass of wine, and a minute later she was talking about something else. But, Johan thought, wasn't Schumann still Schumann, even in the asylum? Or was Schumann Schumann *only* when he was composing music that would survive himself and Clara, and Mai and Johan and everyone else? Wasn't he also completely and utterly Schumann when he was lying in bed or wandering around the asylum in Endenich, unable to produce a single note, with music grinding on and on inside his head? "Oh, if only I could see all of you again," he wrote in his last letter. "Talk to you all one more time. But the road is so long."

For a while, Johan would cross off every single day in his almanac. He wanted to know whether it was Monday or

Tuesday or Wednesday or Thursday or Friday. He wanted to know whether it was warm or cold outside. In Norway, August is both summer and autumn, depending on the temperature, so every day he would ask the nurses what the weather was like.

It was a Thursday or a Friday, definitely Thursday or Friday. Andreas was due to visit him that day, with his pregnant girlfriend, Ellen. Mai had announced this the day before, or maybe it was the day before that.

But now Johan no longer bothered to tell the days apart and had given up crossing them off. It was warm or it was cold; he didn't care. But the nicest and prettiest nurse, Malin with the long blond hair, had told him it was warm outside.

She sat on his bed and told him it was warm. That morning she had put on three sweaters, because she thought it would be cold. But then, she told him, on the way to work she had taken the sweaters off again. First one, then another, and then the third. It was actually so warm that she didn't need anything except her white cotton slip. She looked at him and laughed. The prettiest nurse by far looked at him and laughed, and her laughter was like fresh water. He longed to drink it.

Johan lay in bed imagining the whole scene. Did she walk to work? Was she at an intersection when she peeled off her sweaters? Or did she take the streetcar? Such spectacles never occurred when *he* took the streetcar.

Anyway, it was a Thursday or a Friday, or both. Could it be both Thursday and Friday at the same time? Johan called to his neighbor on the other side of the screen. "Hey, you there, what day is it today?"

He heard the other man stir and mutter the words *too much, this is too much.* Johan cleared his throat.

"Sorry," he said. "My son's coming to see me. I'd like to know what day it is. I don't want him thinking I don't have my wits about me. Forgive me for bothering you again."

"It's Saturday," mumbled his neighbor.

"Thank you."

The man coughed.

"Thank you," Johan repeated.

Later that day Andreas showed up. All of a sudden he was standing in the doorway, looking stunned. Johan tried to sit up. His boil had been freshly dressed, so as not to startle his visitors. The nurse, Malin, said she had done an especially nice job. And now there he was: his son.

"Eight years," Johan said, his eyes filling with tears. He hadn't expected them. Tears were nothing but dramatics. Cheap dramatics.

Andreas nodded and stepped inside, followed by Mai and a young red-haired woman who was introduced as Ellen. Her pregnant tummy was also introduced.

"It's a girl," Ellen said. "We know it's a girl. I was due yesterday." She laughed. "So now I'm just waiting." She rocked her body from side to side. "Waddling and waiting."

"Me too," Johan remarked mildly. "Not waddling, but waiting, like you."

She looked at him quizzically. She didn't get it, so she tried to explain. "No, what I meant was that I was due to give birth yesterday," she said. "I'm overdue now . . . that's what I meant when I said I was waddling and waiting."

Johan nodded. "I see, is that what you meant! Now I get it." So this is Ellen, he thought. A woman who rarely understands but always needs to explain.

Mai stayed in the background and watched. It was, Johan thought, as if she were intent on taking it all in now so she could describe it in detail at some later date.

Why had father and son not spoken to each other in eight years? The reason was unclear. Andreas had once asked if he could borrow Johan and Mai's cottage in Värmland. Johan explained that it wasn't convenient, and Andreas seemed to understand. Some weeks later they had dinner together, and everything between them was fine. The business about the cottage was barely mentioned, and they had an exceptionally pleasant time. That evening Johan even told Mai that he would like to spend more time with his son. One month later, Johan received a letter from Andreas. In the letter Andreas made it quite clear that he despised his father as much as his father had always despised him. The fact that his father would not even allow him to borrow his cottage was simply the last straw.

Johan shook his head. The letter wounded him deeply, but he didn't know what to make of it. They had had a leak at the cottage, and they'd been doing a bit of redecorating. He had explained all that to Andreas, not that he'd owed him any explanation. His son was a grown man. He couldn't just assume that he could borrow the cottage whenever he liked and do heaven knows what with heaven knows whom in Johan and Mai's most private retreat, among their most personal possessions. But really: a leak. Surely even his son could understand that.

Several days after he received the letter, Johan asked Mai to call Andreas. She was better at sorting out matters like this, he thought.

His son said to Mai, "Doesn't my father realize that I want nothing more to do with him? As far as I'm concerned, he no longer exists."

But now here he was, eight years later. As spindly as his father, but with his mother's face. And with a girlfriend on the verge—any minute now—of giving birth. Johan wanted to ask Ellen whether she had ever read Marcel Bavian's short stories. But he restrained himself and tried to smile, even though it was a painful effort. It wasn't the hypocrisy that hurt so much, it was the physical action itself. Lips, cheeks, eyes, so many parts of his face had to be moved in order to conjure up a reasonably convincing smile. And his head. The pressure that never let up was only exacerbated by their presence. When he probed deeper, the pressure turned into a chant, a string of one-syllable words: *get-out-of-here-it's-no-use-I-can't-take-this-I-want-you-all-out-of-here-get-out-get-out-now.*

"Well, here we are, then," said Andreas. "How're you doing, Pappa?"

"Oh, up and down, you know," Johan replied, struggling to keep his hard-won smile in place. It was threatening to crumble, crack, and gape open, like the boil on his cheek. All sorts of stuff was sure to be oozing out of him soon. He fumbled discreetly with the morphine pump. Everybody saw it, but nothing was said.

"Eight years," Johan said.

"Yes," said Andreas.

The two women, Mai and Ellen, sat quietly listening.

"Eight years," Johan said again.

"But now you're sick," his son responded candidly, "and that changes everything."

Johan wanted to ask exactly what had changed. If his son had come here to forgive him, he might as well not have bothered. Reconciliation, Mai had said, not forgiveness. Johan had done nothing that needed forgiving. He turned to Andreas.

"We'd had a leak!"

His son stared at him blankly. "What?"

"We'd had a leak."

"I'm not following you. . . ."

"The cottage. You wanted to borrow it, and I said no because we'd had a leak—the pipes in the bathroom. Flooding. So we had to do some redecorating."

Andreas looked at the floor. "I see."

Johan looked at his son. Wasn't this what he wanted? Wasn't this enough? He was Alice all over again, holding a grudge for years. Refusing to relent.

"You might have told me," Andreas muttered.

"Told you what?"

"About the leak."

Johan shut his eyes. Was this what it was like to die? He opened his eyes again and looked at Mai. Was this what she called reconciliation, this pathetic exchange between a spindly man in his forties and an even spindlier man of seventy? All this banal chatter about a leak at the cottage, all this lousy, rotten pettiness? Johan's eyes moved to Andreas. What was it about his son that made you feel like punching him in the jaw? It was a familiar impulse. Always there, ever since Andreas was a helpless, amoebic child with trembling hands who never dared do anything and was conceited to boot. His classmates had called him Bighead because even though he was a coward he was always boasting and lying. "Some children are simply harder to love than others," Alice used to say. "We'll just have to try harder. He *is* our little bird."

Johan cleared his throat, summoned up the last of his strength, and reached a hand out to his son. He was, after all, no one else's little bird.

"Andreas," he said, "come sit beside me." His son sat down. Johan stroked his hair. "Can you forgive me?"

"For what? The thing about the cottage?"

"Yes, that too. But for not being the kind of father you needed. Can you forgive me for that?"

Andreas turned to Ellen with a question in his eyes. She nodded to him. Andreas took a deep breath and turned back to Johan.

"There's no need. I . . . you don't understand . . . I just wanted . . ." As always, Andreas broke off in mid-sentence, but this time it was in order to lay his head on his father's shoulder, sigh, and dissolve into tears.

As they were about to leave, when they were standing in the doorway saying goodbye, Ellen suddenly had a thought. She rummaged through her purse and pulled out a camera.

"I almost forgot the most important thing!" she exclaimed.

Andreas was ordered to take up his position by the bedside again. He was asked to sit down and take Johan's hand. Mai was to stand behind, like a ministering angel in the background of a painting. Ellen peered at them through the lens and assured them it looked great, especially with the silvery afternoon light filtering through the window. "There!" she cried blithely. "Captured for posterity!"

"Ellen," Johan said, "do you think you could send me a copy once it's developed?"

Ellen nodded, her eyes flickering to Mai. "Shall I send it here or to your home address or what?"

Mai was about to answer, but Johan beat her to it. "Send it to me here at the hospital. That way I can look at it at night before I go to sleep."

Ellen nodded again but pointed to her stomach. "It might be a while—I doubt I'll manage to get the pictures developed before the baby comes. I could go into labor any time now, but I have to be two weeks overdue before they'll even think of inducing me." She gabbled on. "So I don't know exactly when I'll have a chance to send it."

"Whenever you can, my dear," said Johan. "Whenever you can. And don't forget to send me a picture of the baby too."

Ellen looked at Andreas, smiled, and nodded emphatically.

"I'd like a picture of the moment the baby . . ." Johan cleared his throat. "I'd like a picture of the moment your baby turns to you and touches you for the first time. Could you send me a picture like that, Ellen?"

She nodded again, though she must already have been envisaging the difficulties of taking precisely such a picture.

"Ellen," Johan said.

The pregnant girl looked at him.

He nodded at his son, still holding Ellen's blue eyes with his own.

"Stay with him!" he said.

"Oh, yes!" she said, squeezing his son's hand. "You bet I will."

The days that followed found him screaming in pain. But his screams cannot have been very loud, since no one heard them. His head felt close to exploding. He remembered something Mai had once told him about Schumann. As the darkness invaded his mind, he heard a constant *A* note. This was before he came to be haunted by the uncannily beautiful music that he could neither write down nor play. Night and day that *A*, that constant *A*. It was the same with Johan: a humming sound in his head just kept swelling and swelling. He had no ear for music. He could have mistaken it for a dial tone, and the dial tone was high *A*; everybody knew that. *A* for *amor*, *A* for *arsenic*, *A* for *aspect*, *A* for *apple*, *A* for *angst*, *A* for *abracadabra*, *A* for *ashes*. *A* for *Mai*!

"Did you call me?" Her voice came from far away.

"Can't you do something?" he pleaded.

"I'm holding your hand. Can you feel it?"

"But can't you do something, Mai?"

Moments of confusion. Babble. Words all jumbled up. Backward and forward. *Hey, ho! Sing, sing, sing!* Mai's tears. A whisper, a long way off, addressed not to him but to someone else: "He doesn't know what he's saying anymore."

And moments of clarity. Standing in front of the mirror that day in Värmland.

This is my life. This is my . . . life. And in his mind's eye all he could see was a long straight line, like Mai's braid. Was that all there was? Dearest Mai, was that all there was? Not one little curve?

This set him thinking. He wanted a curve. It grows light in the morning, and dark in the evening, and in the course of the day he turns and looks up at the sky or down the road. It makes no difference. But he turns. There is a curve. To turn is to make a curve. An exquisite, consummate movement.

It grows light in the morning and dark in the evening, and in the course of the day he turns.

There.

Now he could sleep. That was what he meant. All he had to do was turn, and then he could sleep.

"Johan."

Mai was standing over him.

"Johan."

He opened his eyes and looked up at her. She was smiling.

"Did I wake you?"

He shook his head.

"Ellen and Andreas have a daughter. Seven pounds ten ounces. Delivered by cesarean section this morning at five past seven. Mother and baby are both doing well. They're going to call her Agnes."

"After my mother," he breathed.

"Yes."

"Good," he whispered, and drifted back to sleep.

More days of babble. Again he hears her speaking to one of the white coats. "He doesn't know what's going on. He's miles away now." Again he hears her weep, and the white coats comfort her. He wants to shout, "No! I'm not miles away. I'm here!" But it hurts and he can't do it. Other sounds escape from his lips.

. . .

One night she comes to him. It must be night, because he hasn't heard a sound for hours. She sits down on his bed.

"Johan," she says.

"Yes, Mai."

"Johan," she says, again.

It occurs to him that maybe she can't hear him, so he opens his eyes and looks at her.

"It's time . . . isn't it?" she asks.

"I don't know," he says. "I'm lying here waiting for it to grow light. Listen: It grows light in the morning and dark in the evening, and in the course of the day I turn. It's as simple as that." He tries to laugh. "It's a sort of mantra. It doesn't mean anything, but if you say it over and over again it helps."

She is not listening. "I think it's time, Johan." This time she isn't asking.

"But I just told you . . . you're not listening."

"I know you better than anybody else," she goes on.

"I don't know about that," he says.

"And we have a language all our own, you and I."

Now look who's babbling, he thinks to himself. A language all our own! Have you ever heard such a thing? Oh, no, Mai. *Maj from Malö*. We don't have any language all our own, you and I.

"Another language," she says.

He stares at her.

"And it's time."

"No," he says. But she doesn't hear. "No," he says again. "Don't, Mai! Not yet! Please! Wait till it grows light."

"I love you," she whispers. Then she takes his hand in hers, moistens his upper arm with a wad of cotton, and injects him with the barbiturate. She sees that he is sleeping and that he is in no pain, that it is good. So she gives him the lethal injection. She watches and waits. So quick and yet so imperceptible. No change in his expression. A trickle of blood from the boil, and that is all. She clasps her hands and says a prayer, not because she's particularly religious, or because Johan was, but because somehow it seems the right thing to do.

She leaves the room, shutting the door behind her, and pulls something from her purse. It is her cell phone. She calls Dr. Emma Meyer at home. This is not the sort of conversation one begins by apologizing for calling so late and waking the whole house, though it *is* late. It is no longer night. Soon it will be light, and Dr. Meyer listens to what Mai has to say: that she's prepared to give herself up to the police. That she's prepared to stand trial. That she has followed her conscience. She made a promise and she has kept it.

Dr. Meyer says, "He was going to die soon anyway."

Mai starts to cry.

"I won't tell anyone about this, Mai, not if you don't."

Mai's voice, surprised, faint: "You won't?"

"No."

"Why not?"

Dr. Meyer is silent. Then she says, "Because you respected Johan's wishes. You knew him; I didn't. Nor did any of those people who would feel justified in judging you if this were to get out."

Mai has no answer to this.

Dr. Meyer says, "Wait right there, Mai. I'm on my way. We'll have some coffee and a sandwich. After that you're going home to get some sleep. And then, a few hours from now, the day can begin."

Mai nods, the way small children nod when they are talking on the telephone, heedless that the person they are talking to cannot see them.

Dr. Meyer's voice again: "Did you hear what I said?"

"Yes."

"Not a word, Mai. There's no point trying to explain. . . ."

"No."

"Are we agreed?"

"Yes."

After her conversation with the doctor, Mai goes back to Johan and sits down on his bed. The door stands open, a band of light streaming into the room from the corridor. He looks just the same. No change yet. She takes his hand to kiss it, but it is cold and she drops it.

She looks around.

There was no point coming in here.

What was it she wanted, to talk to him one more time? To hear him say it was good finally to rest?

She stands up and walks to the door.

Had he still been alive he would have said, "Her tread is not heavy, but she is tired. So very, very tired. She is tired when she lies down to sleep, and when she wakes up she is tired."

Mai shuts the door behind her, not turning to look back.

It grows dark. A deep darkness falls on Johan Sletten's face.

He would have said, "And your hair, Mai, is more beautiful this morning than on any other."

ALSO BY LINN ULLMANN

*"[Ullmann]'s gift is for weaving the banal details of love,
career and family with the mystic world of dreams and
ghosts into one seamless fabric. . . . The hypnotic allure of
the story adds to the reader's eagerness to return to Stella
and share the enigma of her final flight."*
—The New York Times Book Review

STELLA DESCENDING

Stella descends, over and over, in the course of this haunt-
ing novel. She falls from the womb, since her mother gives
birth standing up; she falls for Martin, who delivers her
new green sofa and refuses to leave; she falls ill and eventually recovers; but her biggest fall, the descent that suffuses
her story, is a plunge to her death off a nine-story building.
Memories and observations related by Stella's adolescent
daughter, her curmudgeonly octogenarian friend, three old
ladies who witness her final moments, and finally Stella
herself combine in cryptic and beguiling ways to unravel
the mystery: Playing a lover's game on that rooftop, did she
fall out of her husband's arms, or was she pushed?

Fiction/Literature/1-4000-3094-3

ANCHOR BOOKS
Available at your local bookstore, or call toll-free to order:
1-800-793-2665 (credit cards only).